DARE TO DESIRE

Book Two in the Dare to Love Series

NEW YORK TIMES BESTSELLING AUTHOR

Carly Phillips

To My Readers – For making it possible to do what I love, buying my books, and sharing your love of reading and romance with me online. This one is for you!

Copyright © Karen Drogin 2014
Print Edition
CP Publishing 2014
Cover Design: The Killion Group Inc.

carlyphillipsauthor@gmail.com
http://www.carlyphillips.com

Sign up for Carly's Newsletter
http://www.carlyphillips.com/newsletter-sign-up/

Sign up for Blog and Website updates
http://www.carlyphillips.com/blog

Sign up for Text Updates of New Releases
http://tinyurl.com/pbq4fbx

Carly on Facebook
https://www.facebook.com/CarlyPhillipsFanPage

Carly on Twitter
https://twitter.com/carlyphillips

NY Times Bestselling Author Carly Phillips turns up the heat in her newest sexy contemporary romance series, and introduces you to the Dare family… siblings shaped by a father's secrets and betrayal.

**"One of my favorite reads this year."
HM Ward, NYT Bestselling Author
on Dare to Love**

Quarterback Alex Dare, had it all—an all-star football career and his choice of willing women—until injury forces him into early retirement. When he is offered a ground-breaking position with a rival team, he's intrigued, but there's a catch. He'll be working alongside the same woman he callously hurt when she got too close for comfort. Social worker Madison Evans grew up in foster homes and knows what it means to have-not. She isn't impressed by Alex Dare's wealth or charm. Not since she fell hard for him once before, only to discover she was just one of his too-easy conquests.

This time around Madison refuses to succumb to Alex so easily. But Alex wants Madison. And if there is one thing Alex does well, it's to get what he wants. Can he convince Madison to take a risk and dare to love?

* * *

ONE

Quarterback Alex Dare took possession of the ball the same way he took possession of a woman's body. With skill, finesse, and the absolute certainty he'd score.

Madison Evans watched the man who'd been in her bed the night before on the huge screen in front of her. She'd joined her friends for Thanksgiving dinner, Riley and her husband, Ian Dare, and Ian's siblings. With no biological family of her own, Madison appreciated having somewhere to go. Eating alone in a restaurant on a holiday, something she'd done often, held no appeal.

The football game held everyone's attention. Watching the massive screen, Madison felt as if she were on the field along with Alex, his teammates, and the opposing players. Everyone around her joked, laughed, and ate the delicious hors d'oeuvres their hosts had supplied.

Someone yelled in complaint. Madison glanced at

1

the television once more. A time out had been called, giving her an opportunity to reflect on the whirlwind couple of weeks she'd shared with the irresistible man.

She'd met Alex when Riley had been brought to the hospital a few months ago, but she'd ignored the quarterback with the playboy reputation in favor of the patient she'd been assigned to treat as the social worker on call.

She'd seen him again at Riley and Ian's engagement party, where he'd turned on the charm and begun an all-out sensual assault. Despite her attempts to keep her distance, she'd broken down, given in, and ended up in his bed that same night. He didn't do relationships, and she'd steeled herself for the inevitable quick end, which hadn't happened.

Though Alex played for the Tampa Breakers and lived almost four hours from Miami, he kept his main home in Miami since most of his family was here in town. His apartment in Tampa existed for convenience during the season, when he was either here in Miami, in Tampa, or on the road.

But ever since he'd sweet-talked Madison into his bed, he'd made up for any physical distance in other ways. They'd talked on the phone and texted often, including sexting when he was out of town. And wasn't that new for her? She squirmed in her seat at the arousing memories. Luckily, this past weekend, his team had had a bye week, football jargon for a week off. Which meant extra time in Miami. And with her.

They'd spent enough hours together both in and out of bed that, despite knowing his reputation, Madison's emotions were already involved. Not smart for a host of reasons. If her childhood had taught her anything, it was to keep her feelings locked down tight. She knew better than to get attached to anyone in any capacity. Especially a man like Alex, who didn't do relationships.

She even knew he was uncomfortable that she was spending this holiday with his family, never mind that they'd been her close friends before she'd gotten involved with him. He obviously hadn't thought through the ramifications of an affair before turning on the charm. But chemistry like theirs didn't come along every day. They had amazingly hot sex. Awesome, no holds barred, panty-drenching sex. Something Madison had never experienced before.

Not to mention, he had a sweet side. He adored his siblings and mother, he was protective of his friends, and he could seduce her with a wink and a smile. Then there were the off-the-chart orgasms. She wriggled and shifted positions because just the thought was enough to get her motor running. He was *that* good.

So if she was stupid enough to have developed

3

some feelings for the man, she at least trusted that because of her friendship with Riley and the rest of his family, he'd treat her with care. If not, Riley would kick his ass, and Madison would be all too happy to help.

She didn't believe in love at first sight. If pressed, she'd have said she didn't believe in happily ever after, but as she watched him move on the field, her heart gave an unmistakable flutter, and she knew she was in trouble.

She forced her gaze to the play on the screen. Ball in hand, Alex scanned the field for his receiver. He obviously found the man he was looking for and raised his arm, poised to throw.

The next few seconds were a blur. He faked, ducked, and ran in the opposite direction only to be charged by a massive hulk of a man on his left. He took a hit and was leveled by opposing players on the right. Madison winced at the force of the blow that took him down. As the men heaped one on top of the other, time out was called.

The dog pile took time to sort as each man slowly rose to his feet. All except the player on the bottom. Number twenty-two, Alex Dare, lay sprawled and unmoving on the field.

*   *   *

Alex knew immediately, this hit was different than the others. Things went black for a few seconds too long. Enough to have panic setting in before the blue sky above him came back into view. *Thank God.* But the pain and the nausea were overwhelming and nonstop. And at some point, he must have blacked out. He woke up in an MRI machine, something he was all too familiar with. The enclosed space and loud banging noises didn't help the pain. Finally, they pulled him out of the tiny capsule, and he answered the requisite questions about day and time, doing his best not to puke or move his head even a fraction of an inch.

Damn, he hurt.

He remembered the start of the game but not the score or the hit. Hell, he didn't even remember the ambulance ride to the hospital. Not unusual for a concussion, and he'd had enough of them to know.

They sent him for more tests, and his head pounded with the force of a hundred bass drums. Waves of nausea washed over him, threatening to make him lose his lunch. If he'd eaten lunch. He couldn't recall.

The team doctor and a neurological specialist were waiting when they finally settled him into a private room. Their expressions were grim, and his heart pounded harder in his chest. Physical pain he could endure. What they wanted to tell him? He was deathly afraid *that* he couldn't handle.

The doctors spoke, sharing the news, their words echoing in his brain. He could not afford another hit to the head. One more concussion could lead to permanent brain damage.

Memory loss.

Depression.

Loss of motor control.

Blindness.

The damned doctors used every worst-case scenario they could think of to make their point: *No more professional football.*

A career-ending injury—every player's worst nightmare.

He refused to talk to the doctors and was grateful when they finally left him alone. For the next hour, he stared at the ceiling of the hospital room, the blinding headache and nausea a constant reminder of loss.

He was twenty-six years old, and all he could think was … what now?

* * *

Six Months Later

Alex woke up in a sweat from the same nightmare he'd had for months after he'd taken the life-altering hit to his head. Not only did he relive the moment of impact, the details of which had eventually returned to him, but he actually experienced the searing pain. Six months had passed since that Thanksgiving weekend, and he'd thought that damned dream was behind him. But he should've expected it again now since training had begun for the football season and, along with it, the renewed feeling that his life was over.

He rolled his tight shoulders, the stress of not knowing what to do next eating at his gut. He sat up in bed and stretched. Maybe he just needed to get laid. After all, he hadn't indulged in his favorite pastime in far too long. Problem was, every time he picked up his phone, none of the names listed there appealed to him.

Okay, one did, but he'd burned that bridge. To the ground, if his best friend and sister-in-law, Riley, was to be believed. Considering the way he'd thrown Madison Evans out of his hospital room, he figured his best friend was right. He winced at the memory, self-loathing filling him for how he'd treated Madison.

He remembered the moment as if it had just happened. After the concussion and the battery of tests, the doctors had insisted on keeping him overnight. Riley, Ian, his brother, Jason, and sister, Sienna, had stopped in to see him. He hadn't been pleasant, but they were family. They had to forgive him. His parents had come next, and they'd understood his depressed mental state. The revolving door of visitors had made his head spin even more than the injury. He'd assured them all he was just fine and tossed them the hell out. Pity and concern were the last things he needed. He'd been throwing a big enough party all by himself.

Then *she'd* shown up.

He'd looked up to see Madison standing there, blonde hair spilling over her shoulders, covering luscious breasts he'd had in his mouth and hands the night before. He might've been down for the count, but he could still appreciate a beautiful woman, and this one did it for him. She had from first sight, which was why he'd kept her around longer than his usual female.

But he'd been getting antsy, especially with how close she was to his family, spending the Thanksgiving holiday with them. How stupid was he, fucking where he lived? He had an old man who'd married one woman while keeping another on the side. Was it any wonder Alex had done something so dumb?

The one and only time he'd let a woman close, she'd cut his heart out without thought. He'd sworn never again and thought he'd meant it. Only Madison had broken through those walls he'd erected, fitting in with his life too well, and it scared the shit out of him.

And now? He had no career, no future, and he sure as hell didn't need to be worrying about a relationship of any kind.

"What are you doing here?" he'd asked her.

"I'm worried about you. I came to see if you're okay." Concern filled her big blue eyes, and she started toward him.

He held up a hand to stop her. "I'm fine."

"Riley said—"

"I don't care what Riley told you. I'm not your problem, got it?"

She visibly swallowed hard, the delicate muscles in her neck working up and down. "I thought you might need me."

He managed a harsh laugh. "I've got my family. I don't need you."

"So we're—"

"There is no we, sweetheart. It was fun. Now it's over."

Moisture filled her eyes, and in that moment, he hated himself.

"I forgot," she said. "Alex Dare doesn't do relationships."

"Damned right," he muttered.

She straightened her shoulders, backbone he'd sensed in her from the beginning taking over. "I was foolish for thinking I found someone human and real beneath the façade. You're every bit the man whore the Internet and your reputation say you are."

She started for the door, then turned back to face him. "You're a cold-hearted selfish bastard too." She stormed out, slamming the door behind her.

His head pounded at the noise, and he cursed out loud.

He could admit now that he deserved every word. There was no getting around the fact that until six months ago, he'd been exactly the man whore Madison had accused him of being. He hadn't seen anything wrong with it either. All the women in his life up to that point had known what they were getting into.

Hell, he thought Madison had too, but that's what he got for assuming. But he should have known better. She was different, and he'd always sensed it. Which must explain why he couldn't get her out of his head, all these months later.

No other woman who'd graced his bed ever lingered in his mind. Except for the blonde-haired vixen he never should have fucked. At this point he was sure that concussion had scrambled his brains even worse than he'd thought. But he couldn't deny that the memory of what he'd said to her shamed him, and it'd been a long time since he could remember feeling that particular emotion.

He slid out of bed and took a long, hot shower. He'd just stepped out when his phone rang.

He grabbed his cell from the counter. "What's up?" he asked, answering at the same time he wrapped a towel around his waist.

"Good morning, Alex," a familiar voice said.

"Ian, good to hear your voice." Alex clenched his jaw, still not comfortable with any kind of relationship with his half brother.

For Riley, he reminded himself. Alex and Ian's wife were best friends, childhood friends. He'd do anything for her, including deal with Ian. "To what do I owe the pleasure?"

"Got a job proposition for you," the other man said.

Alex blinked. "Are you seriously asking me to work for the opposition?" Until his injury, Alex had been the quarterback for the Tampa Breakers. Ian was the president of the Miami Thunder.

Half brothers. Rivals. In more ways than one.

"Not to rub it in, but you're a free agent," Ian said.

At least he hadn't used the word *unemployed*. Because with his recent head injury, that's exactly what he was, with no job prospects in sight. "Yeah," Alex muttered.

"Are you available this morning? Your name came up, and Riley thinks you'd be perfect for what we need."

Now Alex was intrigued. "You've got my attention. What time?"

"Eleven at the stadium," Ian said.

"See you then." It wasn't like Alex had anything better to do.

*   *   *

Madison paced the confines of her boss's office in the

Miami Thunder Stadium. Ian Dare was intimidating on a good day. A day that would be defined as one where everyone agreed with Ian. Today wasn't one of those days.

She'd been working with the Thunder for the past month, having given up social work for a hospital in exchange for starting up an exciting, groundbreaking program with the hometown football team.

She glanced at Ian, not happy with his most recent proclamation. "When I took this position, we agreed this program would change lives, right?" Madison asked.

Ian straightened his tie and met her gaze with those steely gray eyes. "It is. We'll be the first football team to institute mandatory post-career education. The Thunder will make sure its players are capable of a successful physical, psychological, and social transition into the real world when their careers end. I don't care if it's one year into their contract or ten."

She nodded. She would be in charge of getting the program up and running, her schooling and work history in social work and psychology providing the perfect background. She'd also thought she'd have a say in whomever came on board to work with her.

Apparently not.

She folded her arms across her chest. "So tell me how bringing the playboy athlete on board gels with those goals?" Then, realizing she spoke of his half brother, she cleared her throat. "No insult intended."

"None taken." The corner of Ian's mouth lifted in a wry grin.

Dark-haired, buttoned-up men weren't her type, but she'd have to be dead not to notice that Ian was one very sexy man and Riley was one very lucky woman.

"I'm aware you and Alex have ... history," Ian said.

"That's a delicate way of expressing it." Ian already knew she and Alex had history.

Madison wouldn't be surprised if Riley had filled him in on the ugly ending. They shared everything.

Madison had met Riley in her former position as a social worker for domestic abuse victims at the hospital. She'd briefly been Riley's therapist and had ended up being her closest friend. She knew why Riley never kept Ian in the dark and respected it.

"You're a professional. If you set your mind to something, I have no doubt you can handle working with Alex," Ian said.

Madison raised her eyebrows. "Do not try and win me over with platitudes and compliments."

"Are you saying you can't work with him?" Ian asked.

Madison laughed. "You must really be used to

people you can bullshit. Now you're trying to challenge me into accepting him."

He grinned, stunning her. "Is it working?"

"What do you think?" Madison let out a heavy sigh.

She was a pro at protecting herself from hurt and abandonment, and as a result, she chose the men she let into her life carefully. They couldn't get to her on any level except sexually. No chance of being hurt when things ended. From the second she'd laid eyes on Alex standing by Riley's hospital bed, she'd pegged his type. Cocky and full of himself. She'd bruised his ego when she hadn't let on that she'd recognized the infamous womanizing quarterback. Why should she? The battered female in the bed had been her only concern despite his sexy good looks.

But months later, when they'd begun their fling— she refused to call it a relationship now—Madison had warned herself that all she was to him was *a game*. And yet she'd allowed her hormones, his charm, and their mutual chemistry to override common sense.

She'd let her heart betray her. And she'd paid for that in spades, she thought, remembering the days of hurt and pain after he'd callously tossed her out of his hospital room, never to be heard from again.

"Who better to co-chair this program than someone whose career has been sidelined by unexpected injury?" Ian's deep voice broke into her thoughts.

"Oh, I don't know. Maybe someone who takes life seriously?" she spat.

But his injury *had* been serious, she knew. She could still hear the crack of his helmet against the ground in the instant replay.

Ian cleared his throat. "He's lost without football. He needs direction. And he's in a unique position to bring perspective to the players you'll be trying to reach. He'd be the perfect person to talk to the league when we're ready to try to convince them to make this type of program mandatory for all teams."

Madison studied Ian closely. His jaw was set tight, his eyes narrowed. Being close to Riley gave her insight into the man. And she knew that before meeting Riley, Ian had wanted nothing to do with his half sibling. He'd resented his father's *other* family, especially Alex.

"Who are you trying to convince this is the right move? Me? Or yourself?" Madison asked.

Ian stiffened, and she knew she was right. "This is Riley's idea, isn't it? She's worried about Alex, and she asked you to offer him this opportunity." Disappointment settled heavily in her heart.

"Every time you speak, you convince me you're the right woman to spearhead this effort. You're intuitive. And you're correct."

"Nice. So Riley threw me under the bus for him."

"You know Riley better than that," Ian said, his tone sharp as he defended his wife. "She gives her loyalty and love to few people, and you're one of them."

Madison blinked. "So why isn't she here telling me herself?" She couldn't help being hurt and blindsided.

"She's home sick or she would be."

Madison swallowed hard. "Do I get a say in this, or is it a done deal?" she asked Ian.

He met her gaze. "You're in charge. You decide who to hire. Ultimately, it's between you and Alex to decide."

But it was clear to her that both Ian and Riley wanted her to give Alex a chance. "I need to think about this."

Ian glanced at his watch. Then he cleared his throat. "You've got fifteen minutes. Alex will be in the conference room at eleven."

"Keep him busy till 11:15," she muttered.

Madison headed back to her office, frustration, anxiety, and more than a hint of jitters in her stomach over the prospect of seeing Alex again. But this meeting was the least of her problems, and she paced the carpeted floor, pondering the real issue at hand. Could she work side by side with Alex, day after day, remembering what it felt like to have him deep inside her body?

She shivered at the reminder, her nerve endings alive and tingling at the prospect of seeing him again.

Despite how badly he'd hurt her, she still wanted him. And wasn't that the worst part? She, who'd trained herself at an early age not to want or need anyone or anything, still responded to the mere thought of Alex Dare.

* * *

Alex liked the Thunder Dome. The new stadium was a hell of a lot nicer than the Breakers' home in Tampa, not that he'd be caught dead admitting such a thing out loud. Still, he couldn't help the disappointment clouding him, being in a stadium and knowing he was unable to play. It was one thing to make the decision with his rational mind, protecting himself from bodily injury that would affect his entire life. Quite another to emotionally accept that he'd lost the thing he loved most in the world. The game had defined him from the time he'd picked up a football as a kid and had carried him through losing what he'd thought was his first love. And he had stupidly thought he'd leave the game on his own terms.

Apparently not.

Alex followed the directions left for him at the guardhouse and ended up at Ian's office. It was the first time he'd come to his half brother's place of business, and his skin itched with the feeling that something big was about to take place, even if he didn't know what *it* was.

He walked in to find the office as imposing as the man himself. Alex and Ian couldn't be more different in personality—Ian stiff and uptight, Alex easygoing and relaxed.

"Thanks for coming," Ian said, extending his hand.

Alex shook it hard. Man to man, he thought wryly and settled into a chair, making himself comfortable. Sitting across from Ian, Alex acknowledged how far their relationship had progressed. They were in the same room and having a conversation. It was huge.

"Before we go into the conference room, I wanted to fill you in on the proposition I have for you."

"I'm listening."

Ian inclined his head. "You must realize that your injury brought to light the deficit in the league as far as preparing our players for life after the game."

Alex stiffened, as he always did when talk of his career-ending concussion arose.

Ian ignored his reaction and went on. "The fact is, you could have continued to play, taken the risk, and down the road, you'd have been dealing with severe head trauma and mental deficits. You were smart enough to step back. Not a lot of guys are."

Alex raised an eyebrow. "You're complimenting me?"

Ian rolled his eyes. "But now that you're retired at the age of twenty-six, what do you plan to do with your life?" He held up a hand before Alex could answer. "Hang on. That question is part of why I asked you here. It's also a question the league should want all players to consider *before* they're injured and forced out of the game."

"Where are you going with this?" Alex asked, warning himself not to get defensive.

Ian cleared his throat. "I plan to institute a training program that teaches the players to think about the future, do smart things with their money, and take informational classes that will prepare them for later on."

Interested, Alex merely studied the other man and waited.

"Did you know seventy-eight percent of retired athletes are broke within two to five years?" Ian asked. Without waiting for an answer, he continued. "Statistics show fifty percent of ex-pro football player marriages end in divorce because couples aren't ready for the pressures of life after the game. So I want spouses involved in preparation and education."

"You've really thought about this," Alex said, impressed despite himself and his lingering resentment of

Ian.

Ian inclined his head. "It's in motion. I have a social worker on board, and I want you running things along with her."

Alex reared back in surprise. "Why me?"

He and Ian weren't close. Ian came from their father's legitimate family. Alex and his siblings were the man's illegitimate secrets. But secrets didn't stay buried, and the explosion, when it had come, had rocked both families deeply. Alex and Ian had remained on opposing sides for ten years.

Until Riley.

Ian cleared his throat. "Why not you? Or should I say, who other than you? You will have the unique ability to convince the players this is important. You definitely have media presence when this goes public. And let's face it, you have nothing else lined up at the moment."

"And there's the asshole I know."

Ian grinned. He fucking grinned, as if he already had Alex exactly where he wanted him.

"Come meet the woman in charge before you make any decisions."

Alex nodded. Why not? He was impressed with the program and interested.

As he followed Ian to the conference room, passing the hall of champions, life-sized photos of past and present Thunder All-Stars, Alex still wondered why Ian had chosen him. But he couldn't deny the importance or brilliance of the program. There were so many ways guys' lives did a one-eighty after retirement, forced or otherwise, that training and preparation would only help.

"Riley's really behind the idea," Ian said as they approached the closed wooden door.

"Way to try and sway me, man."

Ian shrugged. "I do what I have to in order to get my way." He paused and looked Alex in the eye. "So about the woman who will be working alongside you—"

"I haven't agreed."

"About her," Ian went on as if Alex hadn't spoken. "I'm trusting you to be professional."

Alex narrowed his gaze, his internal radar on high alert.

"And to not be a jerk."

"Hey!"

Without replying, Ian opened the door. They stepped into the room, and Alex laid eyes on the one woman he hadn't been expecting to see. The same woman who'd haunted his dreams and sidetracked him from many of his nightmares.

Madison faced him head on. Her shoulders drawn back, golden-blonde hair pulled away from her face, she didn't back down from his stare. She wore a pair of black slacks that hugged her curves and a white silky-looking top that clung to her generous breasts. And those unusually blue eyes frosted over at the sight of him.

"Alex, I believe you know Madison Evans."

Blindsided—and his half brother knew it—Alex strode up to her. He inhaled her familiar fruity scent, which only served as a reminder of the hot times he'd spent breathing her in as his cock moved inside her body. Her effect on him was potent, and even the most common expressions failed him.

"Alex," she said, her cool tone bringing his head out of the desire-filled fog he'd found himself in.

"Hey, Angel," he said, using the endearment he'd started calling her during their brief time together. Another sign he'd had it bad, whether he'd wanted to admit it or not.

Her head whipped up, her eyes narrowing and settling on Ian. "This won't work." She turned to go.

Alex still had excellent reflexes, and he grabbed her arm before she could stride past him.

She glared.

He didn't look away, determined to win this battle of wills. This potential job, which had interested him on an intellectual and emotional level initially, suddenly felt even more important, and *she* was the reason.

"We need to talk," he insisted.

"I have nothing to say."

"Ian's proposition said otherwise."

Madison looked over his shoulder in search of Ian and frowned. "Well, the traitor is gone. No big surprise there."

Smart man, Alex thought. "If I let you go, will you stay long enough to discuss this position Ian and Riley want me to take?"

She let out a frustrated puff of air.

He took that as a yes and released her.

"Us working together is not a good idea, and somewhere in that thick head of yours, you know that."

"Because we slept together? More than a couple of times?"

She set her jaw. "That was a mistake."

Ouch. That hurt, he thought, and filed away the why to deal with later. "I want to know more about this training program and what my role in it would be."

"Why? You can't possibly be interested."

"It sounds more like you don't want me to be interested."

She rolled her shoulders back even farther, stiffening her posture. "You're right. I don't. This is a serious project that could help a lot of people and have far-reaching positive repercussions for years to come. I need a partner willing to go all in. And let's face it, I've seen your staying power. It's nonexistent."

He winced, knowing she was really referring to him and relationships. And she was right. At least, that's how he had been. Six months with nothing to do but live in his own head, had brought changes she knew nothing about.

Eyebrows raised, stern expression on her face, she glared at him as if he were something she'd scraped off her shoe.

In the span of five minutes, she'd insulted him more than anyone had in probably his entire life. So why was he turned on? He shifted his stance in a futile effort to adjust his cock and gain some sort of ease or comfort. Not happening around her, and he knew it.

"I'll give you that one insult because I deserved it."

She wrinkled her nose in confusion.

Good. He liked her off balance. Much better than spitting mad. "Any more and I'll have to take action."

She opened her mouth then closed it again, because as they were both intimately aware, he'd have no trouble following through on his threat.

"Care to tell me what you have planned for this program?" he asked, deliberately all business. He strode over to the chair at the head of the table and settled in.

She obviously realized he was serious because she headed for the stack of folders on the table and sifted through them.

Coming up with the one she wanted, she opened it and glanced down only briefly before speaking. "Football players—anyone in training for prolonged periods of time—live a very regimented life. From what and when they eat to their exercise routine to when to practice and attend team meetings, everything is laid out for them. One injury and everything changes." She eyed him warily from beneath her lashes.

He was surprised she'd still worry about his feelings after how he'd treated her. "Go on. I can take it."

She nodded. "Suddenly they can eat what they want, when they want, and they gain unhealthy amounts of weight that isn't balanced out by the exercise they used to do. Lack of education and preparation result in poor financial choices. Most athletes run through any good money they might have made in a short amount of time. Marriages crumble from the strain. Not to mention, they get bored, and depression sets in. I have statistics, but for now, you can just take my word for it."

He didn't have to. He'd begun experiencing some of it himself.

"What's your solution?" he asked, impressed with

the knowledge she already had regarding the problem they faced.

"Education." She tapped the folder on the table. "All football colleges and universities need to have programs geared to post-career options. It's not enough to offer a finance or business major. They need to target post-professional life. From our perspective, that means we start from the ground up. We contact schools and propose just such an approach. We hire ex-players willing to speak to the kids about the importance of thinking beyond football. And at a team level, we begin to provide all sorts of counseling and training. Nutrition, business classes, psychological counseling. Another goal is to eliminate the stigma of retirement, and to do that, we need to prepare our players for the future." She finished her speech, her cheeks flushed pink and her eyes wide, her passion for the subject evident.

Fuck, she was gorgeous.

He'd seen a similar look on her face before, right before he'd slid his fingers inside her and teased her to climax. He closed his eyes, dragging in a controlled breath.

Wrong time, wrong place. Wrong everything.

He might want to return to where they'd been before he'd opened his big mouth and thrown her out of his hospital room, but she wanted nothing to do with him. She didn't trust him, and he didn't blame her. He needed to win her over before he could let himself even think about sinking back into her body. She needed to see he'd changed, grown up.

And maybe he needed to prove the same thing to himself.

"I'm in," he told her.

"Excuse me?"

"I'll take the job."

She pinched the bridge of her nose. "Didn't Ian tell you it's up to me who to hire?"

Alex shook his head, silently cursing his manipulative brother. "No, I think the plan was to throw us in here like gladiators and see who survived."

To his surprise, she let out an amused laugh.

The desire to kiss the dimples on either side of her mouth was strong. Beneath the table, he curled his fingers into fists, curbing his desire. His frustration wasn't as easily controlled.

"I really don't think we can work together," she said, sobering.

"Then I'll just have to convince you otherwise."

TWO

Two weeks had passed since Alex had come on board. He'd shown up at the stadium daily, ready to dig in and work. To Madison's surprise and disappointment, they shared an office—due to lack of available space, according to Ian. Madison called bullshit, but only to Riley. She wasn't about to start trouble with her boss.

Alex had stepped out a couple of minutes ago. Alone for the first time, she grabbed complete concentration time and stared at the list of speakers she'd begun lining up for workshops. She wanted to run programs dedicated to everything from health and nutrition to finances and taxes. There was one well-known lecturer in particular she wanted to secure, but she had the feeling nailing him down would entail a trip to Manhattan to convince him. He was on the pricier side, but luckily Ian had given them a generous budget to work with, indicating how important this issue had become to him. She wondered if his newfound relationship with Alex was the root of his support or if he just sensed the need in the sport. A combination of both, she assumed.

She pulled up the calendar on her computer, knowing the seminars had to take place during the off-season so as not to overwhelm the players, and she would need to confer with Ian on scheduling.

She was so intent on her work she didn't hear anyone come up behind her, but she knew, the second she breathed in the sexy, musk-laden cologne, who had joined her. Her body responded as if she knew him intimately, which, of course, she did. She didn't appreciate the reminder, her nipples now erect beneath her sheer silk blouse and a pulsing awareness awakened between her thighs.

"Good meeting?" she managed to ask, knowing Alex had come from a sit-down with the head coach and his team to fill him in on their progress so far and what would be expected of the players.

"Yes with some coaches, no with others. They don't want to think about having to pull players for mild concussions, which is part of what we're advocating. It's not just about getting the players educated, it's about getting those in charge to treat injuries with more caution. Not easy when, in their minds, it's all about the win." A hint of frustration edged his tone.

"It'll take time for them to come around," she said.

"Well, it didn't help that some of them behaved like I was their enemy instead of being on the same team."

She winced, knowing how wide the football division was in the state of Florida. She could only imagine the locker room. "That must have been difficult."

"I can handle it. I'm a big boy."

He might not mean anything by his words. In fact, there was no innuendo in his tone. But Madison's mind immediately went to exactly how big the man actually was, and the memory had her squirming in her seat once more. The friction of her slacks against her sensitized body parts was driving her insane.

He settled on the edge of her desk, too close for her peace of mind.

"What are you doing?" she asked.

"Saying hello." His breath ruffled her hair, and she shivered. "And catching up."

This friendly Alex was new. Up until now, he'd perfected being completely professional, but since they shared an office, the underlying sexual tension was ever present. She couldn't inhale without smelling Alex's familiar scent, reminding her of hot, passionate nights in his bed.

She couldn't look up without catching a glimpse of

his dark head bent over notes or his computer, bringing up memories of how she'd tangle her fingers in the long strands of his hair as her orgasm washed over her. The low timbre of his voice echoed through her, causing every nerve ending in her body to tingle with awareness. And they worked really well together, as it turned out, reminding her that their camaraderie had extended outside the bedroom as well.

On day one, when she'd accused him of not having staying power, it had been a subtle dig at his revolving door of women, not his work ethic. So she wasn't at all surprised he'd thrown himself into this job with the same dedication he'd shown in his football career. She didn't need anything to soften her toward him, but had to admit, she admired his enthusiasm for their project and the ideas he'd brought to the table so far.

Still, she'd expected him to leave at five. Instead, he'd stay until seven or eight, always walking her to the parking lot at the end of the day. What had happened to the parties at his house? The constant rotation of friends and teammates who came through his front door for poker, beer, and pizza? The bars with the groupies?

She frowned at the reminder. Maybe he went there afterwards, but he didn't seem like he was partying. At all.

"What's wrong?" he asked. "You're looking at me

funny."

She frowned at how well he read her. "It's just that you're surprising me," she grudgingly admitted.

"In a good way? Or bad?" He leaned in closer.

"Sit back," she muttered. "I need breathing room."

He shot her a knowing grin. "I don't mind being so close to you." His brown eyes sparkled with mischief. "You smell good." He deliberately inhaled, his nose close to the sensitive spot behind her ear.

"Stop!" She slid her chair back from her desk.

Chuckling, he raised both hands in the air. "Fine. Then spend time with me away from work, and I won't push any agenda here."

She raised her eyebrows high. "So you admit you have an agenda?"

A dimple formed in his cheek. "I admit I want to spend time with you. Anything else I say can only get me in trouble." He grinned, surely intending to disarm her. "Let's go for dinner tonight."

"I can't."

"You mean you won't."

"I mean I can't. I have a date." With her foster brother, Eric, but she wasn't about to give Alex any information on her family issues.

His smile turned into a deadly scowl she'd only seen on the football field. Did her after-work plans really bother him so much?

"Who's the guy? Is it serious?" he asked, suddenly back in her personal space.

She felt lightheaded at his nearness, and the desire to throw herself against his hard body was strong. "I'm meeting my foster brother," she said, only realizing she'd buried herself with the truth.

A shimmer of light returned to his gaze. "Okay, eat light with him, and we'll go out after."

She wrinkled her nose in confusion. "What's with the persistence? I mean, if you were anyone else, I'd think you don't want to go home and eat alone." But Alex Dare was never alone.

He looked away and awareness dawned. Could he be lonely? "Alex, what's going on? Where are all the guys who came in and out of your house at all hours when I was there?" He was the most popular guy she'd ever met, never at a loss for company, male or female, whether in Miami or in Tampa.

"Things changed." He didn't turn to meet her gaze.

This wasn't the cocky Alex she remembered. But she wasn't letting him off the hook. "Changed how?"

He was silent for so long she didn't think he'd answer. When he did, he spoke so low she had to strain to hear.

"After the hit, I wasn't exactly in a good place."

She knew that firsthand. She bit her lip, refusing to

snap back a retort because it just might give him insight into how much he'd hurt her.

He glanced up at her, the knowledge already in his eyes. "I was nasty to my family, my friends. I didn't want company."

"You weren't at your best," she agreed.

"True." He grinned, the cockiness back.

For some reason, that reassured her. "And let me guess, not only didn't you want their help, you didn't want their pity."

"Bingo. And after a while, the guys stopped coming by." He shrugged like it didn't matter.

Without looking at his expression, she knew better. Knew him better. Scary, considering a few minutes ago she'd thought she didn't know him that well at all.

She cleared her throat. "What about your siblings? I'm sure they were there for you."

"They were. They are. But if they think I *need* them, they'll smother me."

She shook her head at how easily he dismissed something so precious. "You're lucky you have a brother and sister who care." Speaking of siblings reminded her of her meeting with her foster brother, and she glanced at her watch.

"I don't want to keep you," he said, picking up on her cue. He slid off the desk and walked to his own corner of the room, looking more isolated than she liked.

She was torn over what to do. Being with him outside of work was so dangerous to her peace of mind. Most people she found easy to keep out. Not Alex.

"Walk you out?" he asked.

She bit the inside of her cheek, knowing she was going to regret this and unable to not ask it anyway. "Why don't you come with me? I'm meeting Eric for a quick talk. You and I can go to dinner after."

A grin spread across his handsome face. "Lying to avoid me?" he asked, amused and confident once more.

Ignoring the question, she bent down and grabbed her purse from her bottom desk drawer.

"This sudden invite, it's not pity-based right? Just because I confided in you doesn't mean I—"

"Alex? Shut up and let's go," she said, slinging her purse over her shoulder and walking out ahead of him.

They agreed that she would drive and she'd take him back to the stadium later to get his car. He'd been overly agreeable, as if sensing she just needed any little reason to change her mind. He was right. She wanted to run as much as she wanted to go with him. She was too susceptible to him in general when he was *the full-of-himself athlete* he showed to the world. The more vulnerable man she'd seen glimpses of tonight? He was even more of a risk.

She consoled herself with the notion that she could consider this a business dinner. They could discuss the idea of consulting a public relations firm for their campaign. Alex had been been in meetings most of the day and away from the office, so tonight would be the first chance she had to broach the notion.

"Where are we going?" he asked a while later as she drove to a part of town she normally avoided. But her brother had insisted this was where he wanted to meet.

"A place called Dom's," she said as she pulled into the parking lot Eric had mentioned.

"Well, I'm glad I'm with you. Who the hell sends a woman around here alone?" Alex asked, outraged.

She swallowed hard. From the gang of kids on the corner in matching colors and jackets to the homeless man who'd camped out across the street, it was no place for her to be wandering around. Suddenly she was glad Alex was here too.

They stepped out of the car, and he strode over to her, hand outstretched. "Keys. I'm driving us out of here."

Deciding not to argue, she handed him the set. He pulled her against him, his arm wrapped snuggly around her waist as they strode toward the entrance.

Memories of another time, another place assaulted

her, forcing her to recall the times he'd held her tight for far different reasons, when they were a involved. And how much she'd enjoyed it. His strength represented a security she'd never known, his scent and touch aroused her, and damn him, once again she found herself wishing for more than he was willing to give. She stiffened, holding herself apart from him as much as she could.

They paused beneath a ratty awning that hung awkwardly and broken above them, and Alex opened the door for her to step inside, his hand still strong and reassuring against her back.

As she walked farther inside, a mildew-like stale smell assaulted her, and she regretted this meeting even more.

"Can I help you?" a bored-looking woman asked.

"Yes, I'm looking for—"

"Oh my God, you're *him*!" she said, now bouncing in her platform heels, her large breasts bobbing along with her. "You're the hot football player, Alex something." She batted her heavily made-up eyes at him.

"Oh, for God's sake," Madison muttered.

Alex turned on his patented charming grin. "I can't believe you recognize me in Thunder territory," he said to her.

"Of course I do! You're so much hotter than our

quarterback, but don't tell him I said so," she said, leaning close until her breasts brushed his forearm. Her come-on was clear, despite him having walked into the bar with Madison on his arm.

She'd suffered through being invisible when she was with Alex before. Overly enthusiastic women tended to ignore the girl he arrived with, thinking they had a chance anyway. It was rude and ridiculous, and he'd eaten up the attention. She remembered often feeling pushed aside, but she'd accepted it, telling herself it was part of his life. He'd needed to cater to his fans.

"Thanks," he said, taking a deliberate step away from the ogling female fan. He reached out and squeezed Madison's hand.

She blinked in surprise. This behavior was new. After she and Alex had broken up, Madison had realized she'd been making excuses for him. He'd chosen to let her be pushed aside. He could have handled meetings with female fans differently.

And this time he had. Unsure what to make of things, she cleared her throat, intending to move forward with her own agenda.

"Excuse me. I'm meeting someone. Eric Grayson?"

"Haven't seen him," the woman said without pulling her attention from Alex. Clearly she didn't take his distance seriously.

Madison frowned and glanced at her watch.

Alex turned to her. "He's late."

"Five minutes. Not bad by Eric's standards." She'd give him more time. "Are you sure you don't want to see if she wants an autograph? Her chest is nearly exposed and waiting." Madison winced at how catty she sounded, but the words were out, as was the hurt from the times he'd ignored her in the past.

She didn't understand his lack of eagerness over the attention now and couldn't allow herself to put any stock in its meaning.

Alex narrowed his gaze, concern in his eyes. "Madison—"

Before he could speak, a young guy wearing dark jeans and an old tee shirt, both arms covered in full sleeves of tattoos, strode over.

"I overheard you saying you're looking for Eric Grayson?" the guy asked.

"Who are you?" Alex asked, pulling her against him protectively.

"Are you Madison Evans?" the man asked again.

She nodded. "I am."

Beside her, Alex stiffened, and his fingers bit into her waist.

"Who are you and what do you want?" Alex towered over the other guy, his mere presence an implied threat.

The man pulled folded papers out of his pocket, handing them to Madison. "You've been served," he said, then turned and walked out of the bar.

She stared at the blue legal documents in stunned silence, immediately guessing what they were. "I can't believe him," she said, gripping the papers tighter in her hand.

"Do you want to look at them here or in the car?" Alex asked her in a gentle voice.

She didn't want gentle. She wanted to scream. "I don't have to look. I know what he's up to, that son of a bitch." She slapped the papers against Alex's chest, letting him grab them before she pivoted and left the rundown bar where her foster brother had set her up.

The rat bastard. It wasn't enough his mother was one step from inpatient care, he wanted to take away what she held dear. Well, Madison would be damned if she'd let him get away with it.

Shaking, she headed for the car, ever aware of Alex by her side.

*   *   *

Alex wanted to throttle Madison's foster brother for setting her up and catching her off guard. Since she was angry and trembling, Alex was glad he'd nabbed the keys before the disaster in the bar. Madison was too shaken to focus on the road.

He drove them to his favorite Italian restaurant, a small place near his new apartment and owned by a husband and wife, who Alex had come to know well. Considering he picked up dinner or ate there at least three or four nights a week, they'd sort of adopted him since their son lived across the country.

Madison stewed in the passenger seat beside him, silent and seething the entire trip. He was aware when she opened the documents and scanned them briefly only to roll them up once more in anger. He gave her the space she seemed to need, hoping she'd confide in him while they ate.

He didn't know much about her family or background except that she'd been in and out of foster homes growing up, and though she had a close relationship with her last set of foster parents, she disliked their son, the foster brother she'd been supposed to meet tonight. Alex had no more details beyond the bare basics because that was the way he used to like his affairs. As impersonal as he could get away with.

He glanced over. She was still lost in thought. Her hair was pulled back in a ponytail, giving him a good look at her tightly set jaw. She bit into her plump lower lip, and though she was upset and frustrated, the small act only served to ignite the desire never far from the surface when she was around. She'd always affected him on a sensual level, everything she did making him need her *immediately*. Except at this moment, he wanted to help her through whatever was going on in her life more than he wanted to seduce her. And that was a first for him.

Her silence continued in the restaurant. They ordered, and she returned to fuming quietly. Their meals were served, and she picked at her dish.

"Want to talk about it?" he finally asked.

"No." She twirled her pasta with her fork, playing with her food more than eating it.

"You should. It's the only way you're going to calm down enough to eat."

She narrowed her gaze. "Since when do we do serious talk?"

"Since we're starting over." He was prepared for her digs, and though he deserved it, the reminders of what an ass he'd been hurt.

"Right. We're co-workers now."

He set his jaw. Not just co-workers, not if he had his way. "Come on. Talk." He coaxed her to get rid of the anger inside her.

"Fine. You know I was close to my last foster parents, right?"

He nodded. He recalled her once mentioning that the man treated her better than her real father ever had. He also remembered asking why she was spending Thanksgiving with Riley and Ian instead of the Graysons. She'd said something about not getting along with her foster brother and not wanting their animosity to intrude on the older couple's holiday. He wondered now, as he hadn't then, what she'd done for holidays before her friendship with Riley.

"Daniel, my foster father, he passed away three months ago." Her voice caught as she spoke.

"I didn't know."

She pinned him with a glare but spared him a verbal slap about how he would have been aware had he not pulled away.

Who'd gone with her to the funeral? he wondered. Who'd been there when she'd grieved? And why was he just thinking of these things now? Why had he been so self-absorbed before?

"The problem is that Franny hadn't been feeling well long before Daniel died," she said, interrupting his thoughts.

"What's wrong?"

"She was diagnosed with Alzheimer's." Madison let go of the fork, leaving it to clatter against the plate. "She's going to need to go into a nursing home soon, and in case she isn't capable of making that decision when the time comes, she made me her health care proxy and gave me her power of attorney. Not Eric."

Suddenly the papers on the table became clear. "Your foster brother is taking you to court over her decision."

Eyes glassy, Madison nodded. "He threatened to claim I exerted undue influence over her to gain her trust, which is ridiculous. It's just that his own mother doesn't trust his motives or what he'd do with the house if left to his care. That's her sole reason for choosing me. I know what she wants, and I'll respect her wishes."

Though Alex sensed there was more to the story, he had enough information for now to know what needed to happen next. "We'll fight him," he said.

"We?" she asked, stiffening.

"We." He wasn't going to argue with her about it either. "Do you have a lawyer?"

She visibly swallowed hard. "No. But I can make some calls."

"Or you can let me make one for you. I've got one on retainer."

"Of course you do," she muttered.

He ignored the dig. His wealth had never appealed to her, which, he admitted, had always been part of her allure. Someone who liked him for himself. At least the part of him he'd allowed her to see. He'd kept most of the real Alex shut off, as he always had when it came to most people. Except for the few times he'd dropped his guard.

He folded his arms on the table and leaned forward. "You can Google a lawyer or you can let me call the best. Your choice."

She glanced down. "I can't afford the best."

"I can."

She looked up, gaze narrowed. "Why are you offering?"

"Because I can afford to pay and you can't. And because…" He paused. And forced out the words. "Because, despite what you believe, I care." And he did. He cared about her and always had, which was part of what had sent him running in the first place.

"You have a funny way of showing it." She slammed her hands on the table, shoved her chair back, and rose from her seat.

And here they were. He'd known they'd reach this point eventually, he just hadn't expected it to happen so soon. "Sit down," he said, not looking around to see if they were causing a scene.

"What's the catch?" she asked.

"Why are you so suspicious?"

Her eyes, which had been glittering in defiance, dimmed. "Because in my experience, nobody gives something for nothing in return."

And that, he thought, was sad. She might be referring to the people in her childhood, but he'd been the latest to disappoint her. That truth made him want to help her even more. "No catch, Madison. I want to help you."

She lowered herself into her seat, slowly and obviously reluctantly. But he had her in front of him again. He reached out and grabbed her hand, her warmth seeping into his skin. A shudder rippled through her, telling him she wasn't immune despite the walls she'd erected to keep him out. And she didn't pull away. He allowed those small indicators to give him hope.

She let out a sigh. "Why are you suddenly back in my life, pushing for dinners, wanting to help me, claiming you *care*?"

Her eyes filled, and his gut clenched at the sight, reminding him of her pain-filled expression when he'd callously broken up with her months ago.

"Because I do."

"People who care don't treat each other the way you treated me."

His hands curled into tight fists in his lap, beneath the table where she couldn't see. "I know and I'm sorry." The word came out easier than he'd thought it would.

"You're *what*?" she asked, obviously stunned.

He didn't blame her for being surprised. "I'm *sorry*."

That one word took the heat out of her eyes, and

for that he was glad. After years of people catering to his every want and need, he wasn't a man used to apologizing. He didn't do it often, but he'd needed to do it now, bigger and with more feeling than he'd given her so far.

"I'm sorry I threw you out of my hospital room," he said on a deep breath. "You didn't deserve for me to break up with you that way, and I regret how I handled things."

But not that he'd done it, Madison thought, her heart cracking a little more. Still, an apology from Alex was a big deal and something she'd never thought she'd get. "Thank you."

He nodded. "Now can I call my friend Jon? He's a damned good attorney."

She needed help but hated to take from anyone. Years of being dependent on others for the very basics had taught her to value her independence and ability to care for herself. But this situation wasn't typical, and it wasn't just about herself. Franny had plans for her land that Eric didn't support, and Madison would be damned if she'd let him get his hands on the power of attorney and undermine all the good that could come from those intentions.

Her last foster family was unusual in that they had money. They didn't rely on the state checks, as many of her past families had done. Franny had taken

Madison in because she'd wanted a teenage girl around, and Eric had always resented the attention showered on her. As adults, that resentment hadn't waned. When Daniel had passed away, he'd left the bulk of his money to his wife, but he'd given both Madison and Eric a stipend, something Eric had also begrudged her. The money wasn't much, but the very idea that an outsider could get her hands on family money galled Eric. He was as nasty to her now as he had been as a child.

Eric worked in construction. He'd owned his own company but had driven that business into the ground during the recession. Still, he had powerful connections with people in their town who wanted his resort idea to go through. And he needed the money it would generate to get himself back on top.

He also had his grandparents' substantial inheritance, if he hadn't run through that cash just yet. He meant to get his way. Which meant allowing Alex to pay for top-notch legal counsel was probably a smart move. Not that she liked owing him anything, but there was more at stake than her own ego or sense of independence.

"Okay, you can make the call," she said. "And Alex?"

"Yes?" he asked.

She met his gaze. "Thank you. Somehow I'll pay

you back."

"You're welcome, and I don't want your money."

She wasn't about to turn a gracious gesture into an argument.

"I'll handle it first thing tomorrow morning. Now will you relax and eat, or do you want it reheated first?"

"It's fine." In fact, now that the burden had been lifted somewhat, she was starving. "I'm actually hungry," she admitted.

He grinned and shamelessly watched her eat. She was too ravenous to even care. A little while later, she'd finished off her pasta, and they'd ordered coffee.

"Alex, it's so good to see you!" A tall older man wearing a chef's hat and apron strode over to the table. "My Anna told me you were here. And who is this beautiful woman?"

Alex smiled at the man, then rose to shake his hand and pull him into a brief hug. "Emilio, this is Madison Evans. Madison, this is the best chef closest to my apartment," he said, laughing. "I'm kidding. The best chef in Miami. He's a well-kept secret, and considering how often I eat here, I'd like to keep it that way."

"You flatter me." The chef turned his dark gaze on Madison. "Nice to meet you, Madison." He looked her over, ending his perusal with a warm smile. "I'm thrilled to finally meet someone special. Alex is always here alone, but he deserves—"

"Your crème brûlée dessert," Alex said, interrupting him, for which Madison was grateful.

Neither one of them wanted her labeled as someone special in his life.

"I can take a hint. It seems like only yesterday I wanted to be alone with Anna. Now? A full restaurant makes us happy, and going home at night together makes us content." He strode off toward the kitchen, humming as he walked.

Madison smiled. "He's a nice man."

"One of the best," Alex murmured, his gaze shifting to hers. An unexpected heat darkened his gorgeous eyes.

Madison shifted in her seat. "So what did you mean by your apartment? What happened to your house?"

He shrugged. "I sold it."

She couldn't have been more shocked. Alex loved his house. Had decorated it to his exact taste, and he'd been so proud to own it. "What? Why?" She couldn't believe he'd parted with his gorgeous Star Island home.

"You know that program we're instituting? Post-football planning? Well, even before Ian asked me to help with it, I knew I had to make some serious decisions. I didn't want to worry about not being able to afford the mortgage." He looked away, clearly embarrassed about his change in circumstances.

She blinked, proud of his foresight and the fact that he'd sacrifice. "Alex, I'm sorry. I know how much you loved the place."

He nodded. "I bought it after I signed my first huge contract, but I didn't grow up with that kind of wealth. I mean, my father had it—his house with Ian's mother was a mansion but my mom kept us in the middle-class neighborhood where she felt comfortable. And Dad didn't push because if he bought another huge place, eventually someone would notice him. I'm cool with living within my means and saving for the future."

Warmth filled her chest as she listened to the pragmatic side of him she'd never seen before. She was curious about his childhood, but now wasn't the time to ask. "I think that's brilliant. I know you'll miss the place but—"

"Actually, I don't. It was too big for one person. And it was more for my ego than practical purposes," he said, flushing at the admission.

His reaction only made her like him more, something she didn't want or need, not after he'd offered his help with the lawsuit, something personal and important to her.

"What does your agent say about other kinds of offers?" she asked, knowing he still had to be marketable in many ways.

"I've been one of those asshole clients who didn't want to discuss anything that didn't include playing ball," he said with a wry laugh. "I'm over it now, but I haven't called him since I told him where to shove his last suggestion."

She burst out laughing. "That sounds a lot like you."

He grinned and knocked her breath right out of her chest. It wasn't fair, the effect he had on her. "My agent is a bulldog though. He keeps trying."

She didn't envy him dealing with people like that.

"Aren't you going to ask me about the other thing Emilio said?" Alex asked.

"I don't know what you're referring to," she lied. She knew exactly what he meant. But to talk to him about the women in his life?

No way.

"He said I haven't brought anyone here, and he's right. Maybe you should ask yourself why I brought you."

A frisson of awareness skittered across her skin. "Alex, this is a bad idea. We had our time, and I'm not sleeping with you again." Even if he seemed to have changed, even if she desperately wanted to, she couldn't go there again.

Didn't trust him with her heart. Hell, she didn't trust anyone, but he'd done the most damage in her adult life. She'd told Daniel all about Alex, and he'd wanted to meet him. Then Alex had broken her heart, Daniel had died, and Franny's mind had developed even deeper holes that caused her to slide in and out of the present. Lately she had moments where she didn't recognize Madison at all.

The last few months had consisted of Madison, all alone, dealing with potential loss yet again, and though Alex was the first one she'd thought of for comfort in her darkest moments, he was also the last person she'd ever call. He was back in her life, but if she let him in this time and he reverted to old patterns, she didn't know how she'd handle that kind of disappointment and pain.

He rose from his seat, coming around to slide into the booth beside her. One strong arm slid behind her as he pulled her close. "Here's the thing. I get why you'd say we're a bad idea, but I don't agree. You need someone in your life, and I intend to be there."

She narrowed her gaze. "You really think you've changed that much?"

"Do you call being celibate changed?"

She blinked at that, surprised he'd been so blunt. Shocked to her toes that he seemed to be serious.

"Assuming I believe you, I have to ask why."

His eyes focused on her in an unsettling way. "Because I couldn't get you out of my head." He slid his hand over hers, the warmth giving her a strong sense of security the likes of which she'd never felt before.

One she didn't trust. She couldn't. Except the part of her that had always longed for complete acceptance and a place to belong wanted to believe.

THREE

With his hand on the small of her back, Alex led Madison out of the restaurant. She wasn't immune to his touch. Her body came alive, the tingling traveling from his hand straight through to her sex. It seemed her traitorous female parts were more than willing to lead her astray, and she was amazed at how much she wanted to let them.

Darkness had fallen while they were inside the restaurant, and apparently Emilio didn't splurge on parking lights. Nobody else appeared in the lot, and her car was in a secluded corner, leaving Madison alone with Alex. So now the fates were betraying her too, she thought, as she hit the unlock button on her key fob.

She waited for him to open the car door, her heart pounding in her chest. Instead, he paused at the side of her vehicle, his dark eyes boring into hers.

A quick pivot of his big body and he cornered her against the passenger door, enveloping her in his heat.

His hard thighs pressed against hers, and his delicious scent surrounded her, making the urge to bury her nose in the crook of his neck and inhale strong. She curled her hands into fists to prevent herself from acting on the crazy impulse.

He slid his hand around the back of her neck, tilting her head up so she had to meet his gaze. His expression was one of determination. "I want another chance."

Want filled her every pore. "Alex—"

He shook his head. "I'm not giving up."

She parted her lips—to disagree, she hoped—and he took full advantage, sealing his mouth over hers, stealing her arguments along with her breath. His tongue tangled with hers, and any rational thought fled in the wake of his kiss. She'd dreamed of tasting him one more time, and he didn't disappoint. He took over the same way he always had, overpowering. Demanding. And she gave in to him as if she were meant to be his.

His tongue gliding in and out, his mouth mating with hers, he gripped the back of her head in his hand, holding her firmly as he devoured her like he was starving and she was his ultimate meal.

She squirmed, needing to get closer, and each movement brought her pelvis in line with his but not close enough. Using his foot, he kicked her leg wider and settled himself between her thighs, backing her up against the car. His hips nestled into hers, his solid erection hard and unyielding against her pulsing core. She was hot and ready and wanting him.

And God, he felt good. She arched, and he rocked his hips, enflaming her need further. She moaned at the sensual assault on her and the intense sensations rocking her body.

He nipped her lower lip and immediately soothed the sting with his tongue. "Remember that, Angel? How good we are together?"

Her pussy throbbed to the heat of his words. She remembered. God, she remembered everything he made her feel.

"I didn't hear you. I asked if you remember." He tugged harder on her hair.

"Mmm-hmm. I remember."

"And it's so good, isn't it? So fucking hot?" He ground his dick into her sex. "Like you've never had before?"

"Or since," she admitted. She hadn't been with anyone since him. She didn't know if he understood exactly what she meant, but he groaned at the admission.

The sound triggered a primal need, and desire took over what remained of her rational mind. She gripped his shirt in her hands, pulled him close, and kissed him again. Licking his lips, sucking on his tongue. He tasted a little like the beer he'd been drinking and a lot like the only man she desired.

Heat wound its way through her body, and she melted under the thrust and plunder of his tongue. She'd missed this. She'd missed him.

His hips continued a constant rotation against her pelvis, and dampness flooded her panties, bringing her closer and closer to an explosive orgasm. It wouldn't take much. His unique taste, his masculine scent, and the hard planes of his chest beneath her hands all made her so aware of herself as a woman. Another roll of his hips, his cock so hard against her clit, and she moaned at the delicious waves tempting her.

So close, so close. Another quick swivel of his hips and a jerk of his hard cock and she'd—

Suddenly she stood alone against the car, confused and frustrated beyond belief. "You're playing games?" Her fingers touched her swollen lips.

His eyes darkened. "No way, Angel. Not anymore. I said I wasn't giving up, and I meant it."

"So…?" She spread her hands. "What's up with you stopping?"

He grinned. "Believe it or not, this is me being a decent guy. With blue balls, but whatever. Before that kiss, you were against anything happening between us again. So I'm giving you time to digest the fact that not only are we going to happen, but you're going to want it. When you're not climbing the walls with the need to fuck me, you can decide you want to give us another shot."

She exhaled a shaky breath. "You left me hanging," she muttered, unwilling to address what he really wanted from her.

"I left us both hanging." His voice sounded strained and raw, and for the first time, she realized his restraint was costing him too.

She closed her eyes and blew out a long stream of breath.

His hand slid behind her neck once more, his touch warm and surprisingly gentle.

Her lashes fluttered open as he brushed his lips over hers. "We're not over."

She was very afraid he was right.

* * *

Madison didn't sleep well. How could she when Alex's parting words kept repeating in her brain? Not to mention how she tossed and turned all night. When she was awake, Alex's kiss played in a never-ending loop in her mind. And when she slept? Fevered dreams of her body's response had her writhing under the sheets, needing the completion he'd denied her. She awoke in a sweat, her nipples peaked and hardened, her panties soaked with desire, and despite the battery-induced orgasm she'd given herself before bed, she was still sexually unfulfilled and needy. Which had been exactly his point.

He wanted her to want him. Or at least to admit to wanting him. Which she did, damn the man.

She knew that if she gave in, he'd be an attentive lover. He knew his way around a woman's body, and pleasure was his ultimate goal. Hers before his. She shivered at the reminder of his big, talented hands working her body. Could she keep resisting him if he kept up his sensual assault and deliberate deprivation?

Did she even want to?

She shook her head, knowing she needed more time to think than she currently had, and continued to dress for her coffee date with Riley.

Madison arrived at Starbucks at eleven. She hadn't seen her friend in too long and was glad Riley had suggested they meet up this weekend. Riley's appearances at work had become sporadic, and Madison worried about her friend. She arrived to find Riley waiting for her in the back, two cups on the table.

Madison headed directly for her friend. "Hey, stranger! How are you?"

Riley rose and gave Madison a hug. "I'm good. You?"

"I'm fine." Incredibly horny, but fine. Her situation with Alex wasn't something she was sure she wanted to bring up over breakfast.

They settled into chairs, and Madison took a long sip of her skinny vanilla latte. "Thanks for ordering. This is delicious."

She glanced over to see Riley had a tea bag hanging out of her grande-sized cup. "Where's the Chai Latte you normally love?"

Riley waved her hand in front of her face. "Don't say those words. God." She closed her eyes and breathed in deeply.

Madison narrowed her gaze. "What is going on? Are you okay?"

Riley blew out a long stream of air. "I'm pregnant." Despite her paleness, her eyes gleamed with excitement.

Madison gasped in delight. "What? That's so amazing!" She popped up from her chair and came around to give her very nauseous friend a big hug.

Riley hugged her back.

"No wonder you've been out of the office more than you're in." They resettled in their chairs. "Good thing the boss loves you so much," she said with a chuckle before sobering at the all-too-pale coloring of Riley's skin. "Is the nausea that bad?"

Riley grimaced. "I wake up, and I think I'm going to die or never stop vomiting. Some days I can see how Kate Middleton ended up in the hospital." She placed a hand over her stomach. "The good news is that the doctor says I'm almost at the end of it. If I'm lucky."

"How far along are you?" Madison asked.

"Twelve weeks. Hopefully by fourteen, I'll start to feel human again. I really want to enjoy the experience, but man, nobody warns you about this."

Madison took in Riley's washed-out face. Now that she looked, it was obvious her usually curvy friend had lost weight, and Riley had a knock-out figure.

"I'm sorry. I hope you feel better sooner rather than later, but I'm sure you'll bounce back."

Riley managed a smile. "Me too."

"So how does Ian feel about all this?"

Riley grinned. "Mr. Controlling is even more controlling. He doesn't get that there's nothing he can do to make this better for me. But he's excited about the baby at the end." She caressed her belly. "And so am I."

Madison's heart swelled for her friend. "I'm really happy for you guys."

"Thanks. So enough about me. What about you? How's the job?"

Since they'd already had the discussion about Riley blindsiding Madison with Alex at work, she let it go now. There was nothing to be gained by rehashing it.

"Well, I love the challenge of creating something new. And I have my first meeting with some of the players next week, so I'm going to be getting back into the people part of the job that I miss. So all's well!" Even Madison heard the forced tone of her voice, but what was she supposed to say? She was conflicted and still wanted the man Riley had put her to work with?

"How is it working with Alex?" Riley, ever perceptive, asked.

"I suppose it's too much to ask you to not bring up his name?"

Riley grinned. "No such luck."

"You suck," Madison muttered.

"That's what best friends are for, to ask the tough questions. So … is he getting to you?"

Madison closed her eyes and groaned. Of course he was getting to her. It hadn't helped that she'd seen yet another side to him the other night, a softer, giving side. And he'd *apologized*.

"Yoo-hoo!" Riley waved a hand in front of Madison's face.

She blinked and refocused on her surroundings.

"Okay, I have my answer. That blush on your face and that unfocused look in your eyes tell me everything I need to know." Riley clapped her hands together and squealed with glee. "So things are good?"

Madison swallowed hard. "I wouldn't call things

good. He seems different, but I can't imagine trusting him that way again." She caught the look on Riley's face and rushed on, wanting to have her say first. "Look, I didn't get into a relationship with him the first time expecting anything more than an affair. I knew his history, but there were moments when we seemed to be ... *more*. And even if he wasn't ready, how he broke things off?" She shook her head. "That I never expected, and God, it hurt."

She placed her hand over her stomach and the remembered pain. There was something inherently gut-wrenching about feeling abandoned. It did something to Madison she didn't know how to get over.

How could she? Any time she felt it, she went back in time. Her father had taken her to the mall for school clothes, a rare occurrence in and of itself because he could rarely afford new things. And then he'd left her there, never to be heard from again.

Her throat swelled at the memory, and she cursed Alex for bringing that horrific moment in her life back in Technicolor *again*. That's how she'd felt when he'd dismissed her like she was garbage after she'd come to see him at the hospital. If he'd called her soon after, she'd have chalked it up to his own pain and disappointment over the events in his life and forgiven him. But he hadn't.

"Hey." Riley put her hand over Madison's. "I'm not going to minimize what Alex did. I'm not going to tell you he wasn't an asshole, because he was. I'm also not going to ask you to give him another chance, because only you can decide if he's worth it. What I will say is that I notice a difference in him too."

"Really?" Madison hated the hope in her voice.

She hated that her feelings for Alex were still strong enough to put it there. "I thought I noticed small things in our short relationship that indicated he was different with me, but I realized afterward I'd been delusional. The stereotypical female who wanted to be the one to change a guy who couldn't be changed," she said in disgust.

"Unless the career-ending injury accomplished what you couldn't back then," Riley said carefully. "What if those things you noticed about the two of you *were* real and now he understands what he had—and lost?"

Riley waited, both patient and silent, as Madison digested her words. "You're saying maybe he has changed. And maybe it's permanent."

"I'm saying you won't know unless you open yourself up to possibly being hurt again." She shrugged.

"Why would I do that?" Madison asked.

"Because when you trust and it works out, the payoff is more than worth the potential pain." Riley smiled and patted her still-flat but pregnant belly.

Madison shook her head, unable to fathom being hurt that way again. Sex? Yes, she was tempted to give in and sleep with Alex again, but trust him—or anyone—with her heart? Not happening.

But ready or not, she had to deal with the fact that she and Alex had unfinished business.

* * *

Madison tried to visit her foster mother at least once a week, and she stopped by not long after receiving the legal papers from Eric. Luckily, she and Eric kept very different schedules, and she rarely ran into him. This week's visit hadn't been an easy one. The live-in health care aide agreed it was time to move Franny into a nursing home. Someplace where she could be monitored constantly.

When lucid, Franny agreed and had already chosen the particular nursing home. They'd been waiting for an opening, and there was one now. Although Franny still had days where sometimes she would know where she was, more times than not, she lived in the past. Madison would begin a conversation only to have Franny pick up the thread, except she'd be talking to someone else. Someone from her childhood or early days of her marriage.

The illness was stealing the older woman piece by

piece, and putting her in a home felt like the final stage of loss. On top of Madison's foster dad's death, Franny's memory lapse was yet another blow. But moving her was the right thing to do. Of course, Eric was fighting that too, not wanting his mother to be *locked up*, in his words.

In this, Madison wanted to believe that Eric was looking at his mother as a son afraid to make the wrong choice. He feared she'd wake up and, in a rare lucid moment, be lost in her strange surroundings. Madison was more afraid she'd burn the house down one night while the aide was asleep or wander off when no one was looking.

A week after Madison had been served with legal papers, she met with the lawyer Alex had recommended. He'd made time for her right away, and she appreciated Alex using his connections to get her in.

Not long after she checked in with the receptionist, a tall, dark-haired man strode out into the lobby to greet her.

"Ms. Evans?"

She rose to greet the attorney. Jonathan Ridgeway, Esquire, was a good-looking man with warm eyes and a genuine smile. Madison immediately felt comfortable with him. She knew this whole ordeal wouldn't be simple or easy, and she was glad this lawyer didn't put her on edge.

"Hi," she said, extending her hand, which he briefly took.

"It's good to meet you, Ms. Evans. But I prefer to dispense with formalities. Is it okay if I call you Madison?" he asked.

She nodded. "Of course."

"Then please call me Jon. Did you bring the papers?" he asked.

She dug the documents out of her purse and handed them to him. "I also brought the power of attorney and health care proxy. There are other copies filed with my foster mother's lawyer."

Jon accepted those as well and gestured for her to sit.

She eased herself into a chair across from his desk. She was nervous as she waited for him to read through her papers and shifted uncomfortably in her seat, taking in his diplomas and wildlife photographs around the room.

Someone knocked on the door, and the sound of it opening had Madison turning in her seat.

"Did I miss anything?" Alex asked, walking inside as if he were expected before shutting the door behind him.

"What are you doing here?" she asked, stunned to see him.

"Good morning, Angel."

She shivered at the nickname, the sound rolling off the same lips she'd been recently kissed by. Ignoring the sexual tension at work was nearly impossible, and she felt it again now—the subtle tremors in her stomach and the overwhelming feeling of need she experienced whenever Alex was near.

He glanced at his friend. "Jon. Thanks for making time for us."

"Alex? Why are you here?" she asked again.

The attorney rose to his feet. "Should I give you two some time alone?"

"Yes," she said.

"No," Alex countered before searing her with a determined look. "I said we'd handle this, remember? *We.* I'm here. I would have made it sooner, but I got caught in traffic." He strode around her and settled into the chair beside her.

"Is there a problem?" Jon asked her.

Madison swallowed hard. "No, no problem." She didn't wish to make a scene, so she'd let him stay.

But if Alex thought just because he was paying for the lawyer that he had a right to be part of her personal business, she planned to set him straight later.

Jon refocused on the documents she'd given him, and Madison turned her attention to Alex. He still wore his hair on the long side, but on him, it worked. He sported a button-down shirt and jacket, filling out the material like it had been cut for his broad frame. Just last night, she'd dreamed of the tattoos beneath, covering his tanned skin.

Madison's mouth grew dry. He'd shaved, and his smooth cheeks made her want to press her lips against his warm skin and breathe him in. She could already smell his cologne, and the scent did things to her that should be illegal during the day while she was fully dressed.

He met her gaze, caught her staring, and his lips turned up in a sexy grin.

Before she could react, Jon spoke, breaking the silence. "I take it you want to fight to hold on to the rights assigned to you?"

She forced her gaze to the lawyer and nodded. "It's more complicated than it looks. My foster mother's house is located on property that is surrounded by land owned by the town. It's been in the family for generations and has been zoned in as a private residence, but with Franny—that's my foster mother—suffering from Alzheimer's, she specifically told me when she's no longer able to make decisions, she wants to go into a home. And she wants to sell the house and have the land dedicated to the town so they can turn it into a rec center for needy kids.

"Why didn't she handle this when she was capable?" Jon asked.

A logical question. "Because she was always busy with charity and other things, and she never got around to doing it while she was lucid. No attorney would say she's in her right mind now and change her will. Apparently, Eric, my foster brother, has a deal in the works to sell the land the house is on to a corporation wants to turn it into an exclusive resort on the edge of town."

Jon took notes as she spoke. Beside her, Alex listened intently.

"Go on," Jon said.

"Eric claims he wants to enhance the beauty of the land, but that's not it. He had a drug problem as a teenager, and he's always run with a fast crowd. Wealthy people, parties with cocaine hidden but available." She shook her head in disgust. "Anyway, Eric needs the cash influx the resort would provide. He has an inheritance from his grandparents, but he tends to blow through money and likes get-rich-quick schemes with his wealthy friends. There's no financial interest involved for me. It's about fulfilling Franny's wishes. That's all." She twisted her hands in her lap until Alex reached over, stilling her with his calming touch.

Unfortunately, his touch also worked to arouse her, and she squirmed uncomfortably in her seat.

Jon cleared his throat. "Okay. According to this,

he's accusing you of exerting undue influence on his mother. How so?"

Anger grew once more at the unfair accusation. "I have no idea how his mind works. All I know is I spend more time with her than he does. I'm sure he's going to claim I pressed her into making me her power of attorney. It's just not true," she said, getting worked up at the thought.

Alex squeezed her hand harder in reassurance that he was there. Solid and beside her.

She forced out a calming breath. "Eric has always resented the very air I breathed, from the minute I came into that house."

Jon glanced at the papers. "When was she diagnosed?"

"About a year ago. Her husband was her power of attorney and health care proxy before me."

"She changed it after he died?"

Madison nodded.

"After she'd already been diagnosed," Jon said grimly.

"Yes."

Jon blew out a breath. "When did your foster brother find out?"

"When Franny started talking about going into a care facility."

The other man made notes then asked, "Were you

their only foster child?"

She shook her head. "There were others in the past, but I was the only one who stayed on. Others were transferred out quickly."

"Hmm. I'd like to get my P.I. to do some digging. Maybe we can get something on him that'll scare him enough to make this go away easily. Let me see what I can turn up. Okay with you?"

More money she'd owe Alex if she agreed. "Umm…"

"Whatever you have to do," Alex said.

Jon looked to her for confirmation, and she nodded, both resigned and grateful at the same time.

He rose from his seat, and both she and Alex did the same. "I'll take things from here," Jon said. "I need you to send me a list of people who saw your interaction with your foster parents when you lived there, possible witnesses for us and for them."

"I'll do that. Thank you."

Jon smiled at her. "Do your best not to worry, okay?"

She nodded. "Thank you. Franny was really good to me. I just want to do right by her."

A few minutes later, they were out in the hall by the elevators. Madison decided not to call Alex on showing up today. How could she be angry when he was behaving so thoughtfully? She appreciated having someone by her side even if she had to constantly remind herself not to get used to it.

"Ready to go back to work?" she asked as the elevator door opened and they stepped inside.

The large doors slid shut.

"Actually, I think we should call in sick."

"What?"

"Play hooky. Take the day off and do something fun."

She raised an eyebrow, considering his words. "Like what?" She couldn't believe she'd asked him that. Why wasn't she just saying no to doing anything or going anywhere with him?

"Somewhere you can forget about your problems and relax."

"But we have work to do." And she couldn't imagine taking time off … with him. She'd be too tempted to act on her desires. Her willpower if he even touched her was nonexistent.

"Look, we're going on a business trip in a few weeks. We'll be working then. A day off isn't too much to ask. Besides, I'm related to the boss." He tapped her nose playfully.

"If I recall, your relationship with him isn't the most stable. Are you sure you want to test his temper?"

Alex shrugged. "I also have an in with his wife."

Madison rolled her eyes. "Way to go, using your friendship with Riley to get what you want."

"Whatever works, Angel. Whatever works. Are you with me?"

She hesitated but had to admit it was tempting. Not just the time with him but the day of freedom. She never played hooky, always took her job seriously. Earning money had always come before anything else.

"You, me, the sun, the pool," he continued with his litany of temptations. "I'll even get you one of those fruity drinks with an umbrella in them. Come on, what do you say?" He bumped her hip with his own.

His playful touch sent a shock of electricity shooting straight through her body. She couldn't deny she liked this mischievous side of him, and after a morning in a lawyer's office, she was tempted to allow herself time to let loose.

The elevator doors slid open to the lobby, and the bright sunshine from the glass doors beckoned to her as they stepped out.

She felt his questioning gaze on her. All he'd asked for was a day off to have fun.

She didn't need to overthink this. "Okay. We can go."

"Really?" He grasped her shoulders and turned her to face him.

His eyes lit with pleasure at her agreement, and she wanted to keep the sparkle there.

She nodded. "Now let's go before I change my mind."

*   *   *

Ian had lived well before he'd married Riley and moved out of downtown Miami. His apartment was an offshoot of The Ritz, a condominium with all the amenities of a hotel. The perfect place for Alex to bring Madison for a day off, one they could spend together. He thought it was a brilliant idea when he thought of it.

Now, as he watched Madison peel off a silky top to reveal the bikini beneath, he wondered if he'd thought this through enough. Lavender-colored ruffles covered her breasts, and a matching bottom barely concealed everything else. His mouth grew dry at the sight, the idea of tugging on the strings and revealing that luscious body to his hungry gaze all he could think about. He adjusted himself as discreetly as possible in his swim trunks.

It being a weekday, most people were at work, and other than another couple at the far end of the pool, they were alone. Alone with thoughts he shouldn't be entertaining for a woman who was still playing it cool with him.

"I didn't realize Ian kept his apartment after he and Riley moved to their new house," Madison said. "It was nice of them to let us hang out here. And on a work day, no less."

"Perks, Angel," he reminded her.

"Something tells me you only asked Riley for permission," Madison said.

He grinned. "I'm connected, not stupid."

She burst out laughing, the first freely given laugh since he'd seen her again in Ian's conference room, and he soaked in the joyful sound. Damn, he had it bad.

He'd driven her home to drop off her car and let her change clothes before stopping by his place to do the same. He'd called Riley for permission while Madison was getting her stuff together. They'd then headed here. Thanks to the confined car, he now knew she smelled of peaches and cream, and his cock had been at attention ever since.

He hoped seducing her was the answer to this all-consuming need, because he didn't know what else would satisfy him. Nor did he know how long it would take to achieve his goal. At the thought of sliding into her wet heat again, he stiffened even more. He raised his knee up to deflect attention.

She lay down on the lounge chair and clipped her hair up, revealing her slender neck. His tongue begged to run down the smooth skin.

Slow down, asshole, he cautioned himself. Where Madison was concerned, he had a lot to prove. So he'd wait her out and would be here on her terms.

For as long as it took.

FOUR

After an hour under the blazing hot sun, watching Alex in swim trunks, his tanned six-pack glistening with sweat, those tattoos looking delicious enough to lick, Madison was ready to cave in to every carnal desire running through her mind. And she'd had plenty.

Needing space, she rose and headed inside the cabana behind them. She dug through her bag for a bottle of sunscreen and sat down on the recliner inside to apply it. She'd finished her face and arms when a shadow loomed in the entryway.

"Need some help?" Alex stepped into the cabana, taking up the rest of the small space and what remained of the oxygen.

"I've got it."

He settled in beside her. "But where would the fun be in that?"

He took the bottle from her and poured a liberal amount of cream into his big hand. She wanted to suggest they go back outside, but they were almost equally secluded there, and she needed a break from the intense heat of the sun.

"Lie back," he instructed.

She tensed, sensing this was a turning point. If he put his hands on her, she was done for. But it was her decision to make, and she had to choose whether to trust him enough to let him back in.

She thought about Riley's words. *You won't know unless you open yourself up to possibly being hurt again.* Seeing Alex at the lawyer's office, so compassionate and interested, made her want to try again. She had to ignore those urges. But her desire to sleep with him? To have mind-blowing sex and quell the need he inspired? Well, that she was ready for. Granted, she was no expert on sex without emotion, but she had no choice. She remembered the pain of heartbreak and abandonment all too well. So this time, she'd keep her head and her heart protected, and she'd be the one to walk away first.

So she lay against the back of the chair, stretching out completely. He gripped her foot with his big hands and began massaging the coconut-scented cream into her skin. Oh yeah, she was so done for. She tipped her head back and moaned, his sensual massage feeling so unbelievably good.

This was no sunscreen application, and they both

knew it. His thumb pressed deeply into her arch, abused from wearing high heels all week. She sighed in delight as he worked first one foot, then the other. His talented hands slid up her calves and pressed into muscles she'd pulled on the treadmill at the stadium. He released the pressure that was always a part of her, and she reveled in the relaxing feel. Somehow she managed to maintain a dispassionate distance as he worked her lower leg, massaging from her toes to her calves and up above her knee. But too soon, his hands lost their greasy feel, and his roughened fingers now slid over her skin, beginning a slow climb up her thigh.

The change in sensation caused a pulsing in her lower body, and she moaned, the sound echoing around the enclosed cabana.

"You have no idea what that sound does to me," he said in a gruff voice.

This was what she wanted. Arousal. Mutual pleasure. And she gave in to his now tender yet seductive ministrations. "Keep working, cabana boy," she murmured without opening her eyes.

"Cute," he muttered, inching higher, his hands splaying over her upper thigh, mere inches from the edge of her skimpy bikini bottoms.

She held her breath in anticipation of his touch on her sex, of his fingers sliding over her moist heat. But he stopped, his fingers curling into her flesh with just a little bite. He liked it that way. Just a little rough, showing her how good a hint of pain mixed with pleasure could be, and her nipples hardened at the memory. Desire further dampened her bottoms, need pulsing in a steady beat between her thighs.

"Angel." The one word sounded like a command, and her heavy lids snapped open, automatically responding.

"Let's be clear," he said in that sex-personified voice that turned her insides to mush. "This is about you. I'm not asking for anything in return. Not even for you to trust me again."

She hadn't expected conversation or discussion, nor did she want any. Hot and fast sex, no time for thinking. That was normally his style anyway, so she didn't anticipate a problem being able to convince him.

"No talk, just work," she reminded him, keeping her tone playful.

"Not until you really hear me. *This*"—his thumb took one swipe over her sex, unerringly finding that hardened nub of desire beneath the bathing suit—"is about you. The rest we'll take one day at a time."

He pressed down harder on her clit, the pad of his thumb connecting with the exact spot that craved his touch.

She arched her lower back, her hips rising of their

own accord.

"Understand?" he asked.

"I can't think when you're touching me."

His low chuckle enflamed her even more. "All I ask is that you take us one day at a time, starting now."

"There is no us. You don't really want that anyway." She reminded him of who he really was.

His gaze darkened, his sexy jaw set in frustration. "Baby, *this* is something."

"*Baby*, this is sex," she said, amazed she could speak, let alone maintain the train of thought that demanded she hold on to her heart.

His shocked expression was priceless. If only she could snap a picture and remind herself that, finally, she held the upper hand.

"So that's how you want to play it?" he asked, his fingers tightening incrementally.

She wondered if she'd see his indentations on her skin later, knowing there had been nights when she'd gone home and examined the reddened prints and remembered the desire that had fueled each one. He wasn't into kinky sex, but he did like her to feel him the next day.

"You wrote the rules," she reminded him. She was just the one who'd forgotten to believe them. "Sex not romance," she said, echoing words he'd used the first time they were together.

He shook his head, amazement in his handsome face. "Be careful what you wish for." With a low growl, he pulled at her bikini bottoms until he'd slid them down and off her legs, dangling each over the edges of the chair. Open wide to him, her pussy throbbed with need.

On a mission now, he slid his hands over her stomach, down to her damp outer lips. "You're so damn wet for me." Gruff pleasure sounded in his voice.

He lowered his head, and she braced for his mouth on her *there*. Instead, he pressed his lips to her stomach, nuzzling her with his mouth, licking her skin. Her belly rippled, even more moisture seeping from her core. Soft kisses, so at odds with the harder side of him she knew existed, told her he had an agenda. One that would frustrate the hell out of her while letting him enjoy every minute.

His tongue swiped from belly button to the top of her sex, and she gripped the arms of the chair in both hands.

"Need something, Angel?" He raised his head, his gaze meeting hers. A sexy grin edged the corners of his mouth.

She stared back defiantly.

"No? Okay then, slow and steady works for me. *Seduction* works better for me."

Gaze never leaving hers, he slid his thumbs back over her outer folds, and her breath caught in her throat. Then he lowered his head and licked her thoroughly, his tongue laving her inner and outer lips, tasting and teasing along either side of her clit, never quite touching her where it would do the most good.

She rolled her hips beneath him, and he slapped her thigh lightly. "Hold still."

"Can't." His talented tongue felt so amazing, and everything inside of her was coiled tight, waiting to explode. But instead of sucking on her clit like she needed him to do, he continued to lap at her everywhere else. Licking, tasting, *teasing even more* until Madison threw her head back and moaned, the sound echoing in the dark, enclosed space that smelled of musky coconut and, yes, sex. Even the air vibrated with desire.

He slid one finger inside her, still not touching her throbbing center that begged for attention.

"Oh God." He thrust one long digit in and out, filling her and yet creating an even bigger ache than before.

He added a second finger, drove in and out of her pussy with relentless strokes.

"Please, Alex." Now she wasn't above begging.

"Please what, Angel?"

"More, harder, faster." Her legs shook, thighs

trembled. She thrashed beneath him, and still he took his time, thoroughly making a meal out of her with his mouth and tongue, fucking her with his fingers.

"Oh my God! Do something, Alex. Make me come."

He finally listened. He clamped his lips over her clit and nipped her hard. Stars flashed in front of her eyes, and she came so fast fireworks exploded inside her head. Waves of pleasure crested, peaked, and washed over her in never-ending swells. She arched her back and gyrated her hips against his mouth until she collapsed against the chair, lost to everything around her.

She came back to herself, expecting to see him naked above her. At the thought, her pussy contracted once more. Instead, she found him watching her, his eyes glazed with desire, lips damp with her juices, a satisfied expression on his face.

"That was fucking hot."

She crinkled her eyes. "Aren't you ... I mean, aren't we going to—"

"I said this was about you." He shifted beside her, the bulge in his bathing trunks obvious.

"But—"

He placed a finger over her lips. "I plan to show you I'm a man of my word. You can believe what I'm telling you I want. And I want you to trust me. I want more than just sex."

Her heart pounded hard, and she shook her head hard. "No. I can't go there again. This is sex, Alex. Nothing more." The lie caused a painful ache in her chest.

He didn't know what it meant to be in a relationship, to give to someone and not walk away when he was bored, finished, or ready to move on. But she knew what it was like to be left. Too many times to count.

She bit her lower lip, and he slid his thumb along her pouty mouth. Her breath caught in her throat.

His gaze darkened. "We'll see."

She shook her head, licking the pad of his thumb at the same time. "Has anyone ever said no to you?" she asked, hoping he didn't notice the tears of frustration in her eyes, the pain in her voice for the things she wanted but could never have.

"Not when it mattered," he said, his honesty surprising her. "And you matter. I also know how to work for what I want. And Madison?" He looked directly into her eyes. "I want you."

* * *

After dropping Madison back at her place, Alex headed home to shower and jerk off. He had no choice, considering how worked up he was after their afternoon together. He'd finally gotten his hands on her again, and it was as good if not better than he'd remembered. Once she let go, she was vocal with her needs, and those barriers she liked to keep so high were almost nonexistent. But she still didn't trust him, and damned if he knew what direction to take next.

He needed to get out tonight, so he called Jon to meet him for dinner. The lawyer was one of the only friends who'd stuck around after his injury. Alex might have been a nasty SOB for a while, but true friends didn't bail. A couple of his other buddies lived in Tampa when they weren't on the road, and most of his childhood friends only stuck around when times were high and fun. Once good-natured Alex had disappeared along with the career and the status, they'd drifted away too. He and Jon were childhood friends, and they'd gone to University of Florida together. Their bond was tight.

They planned to meet up at their favorite steakhouse and grab their usual seats at the bar. Alex got there first. Nick, the owner and bartender, cleared seats for them when they called ahead. Though Alex had cut back, there were perks he didn't mind spending on, and this was one of them.

He was sitting on a barstool waiting for Jon and watching baseball when he heard his name. He turned to see Ian walk up to him.

"Hey. What are you doing here?" Alex asked, surprised to see his half brother downtown. His new house was outside the city.

"Riley was craving steak, so I said I'd stop on my way home. How about you? Having a drink?"

"And dinner. Waiting for a friend."

"Madison?" Ian smirked.

Asshole. "No. I dropped her off at home earlier."

Ian grabbed the barstool beside him and made himself at home. "Enjoy your day off?" he asked.

"Actually, we did."

"I heard you two are going to New York City on a business trip."

Alex nodded. Business was a safe enough subject with Ian. "There are some lecturers she wants to interview, and I'll start making inroads with the Giants coach. Gauge interest."

Ian nodded.

"I also figured I'd meet up with Gabe." Their grandfather, their father's father, had a brother, who was Gabe's father. Both older men were in the hotel business, and Gabe's dad had left Miami to take his business to Manhattan.

The family situation had been awkward for years after the revelation of Robert Dare's other family. But the relatives had reached out to Alex's mom and the kids, welcoming them, and Alex had a close relationship with Gabe.

"I heard he's thinking of opening another club," Ian said.

Alex nodded. "Gabe loves a challenge."

Ian rested an elbow on the counter behind him. "Speaking of Madison—"

"We weren't." Alex scowled.

"Are you making any progress on that front?" Ian asked, ignoring him.

Since the smirk didn't leave the other man's face, Alex wasn't sure how to take the comment. "Are we really doing this? Discussing my love life like you give a shit?"

Ian shrugged. "Maybe I do."

That gave Alex pause, and he lifted his beer for a sip, assessing the other man and deciding to take him at his word. "Progress comes in many forms."

Ian nodded and gestured for the bartender. "Macallan on the rocks," he said to the man.

"Put it on my tab," Alex called out.

Ian cocked an eyebrow, then nodded. "Thanks."

"No problem."

"Riley's worried about Madison," Ian said.

Aah. Now the inquisition made more sense. "I'm not going to hurt her again."

"Good because apparently she had a rough child-hood. I think that's why she and Riley bonded so quickly."

Alex muttered a noncommittal response, not wanting to admit to Ian that he knew less about the woman he cared about than he'd like. He'd been such a self-centered asshole before. Alex shook his head in disgust.

"What?" Ian asked.

Alex didn't plan on elaborating on that. "You're probably right. Both their childhoods sucked. Riley's father was an abusive asshole, and Madison grew up in foster care."

The bartender set Ian's drink on the counter and discreetly walked away.

Ian raised his glass. "Sucks to be left by a parent in any manner, but who the fuck takes a kid to the mall and leaves her there for good?" Ian shook his head and took a healthy swig of his drink.

Alex choked on his beer.

Ian's eyes opened wide. "Oh shit. You didn't know?"

Alex pulled in a deep breath. "No. Can't say I left many openings for her to confide in me the last time we were together." Admitting his failings out loud sucked, but somehow, at the moment, it felt right.

Alex loved his younger siblings, but they were closer with each other than with him. Mostly because football had occupied all his time. He knew that explained why he'd sought a bond with Ian when he'd discovered he had a sibling with whom he had something in common. He needed to change the situation with his brother and sister. Just like things were changing with Ian.

Ian slapped him on the back. "Give it time. It isn't easy to change. Ask Riley. Hell, ask me. We were both closed off before we found each other."

Alex rolled his stiff shoulders. "Madison doesn't want get-to-know-you time. She just wants sex," he muttered, staring at his beer bottle.

Ian burst out laughing.

"What's so funny?"

"If you could only hear yourself, complaining that Madison only wanting sex is a bad thing," Ian said, still chuckling.

Alex scowled. "This time around, I want more."

"And she's making you work for it?"

He shook his head. "She doesn't play those games." And that was the problem. Madison meant what she'd said. He'd hurt her, and she'd withdrawn into herself, unwilling to give him a chance to do it again.

At least now he knew more about what made her tick. "Her old man really abandoned her in a shopping mall?" he asked, his stomach churning at the notion.

A little blonde girl, crying, searching for her father

in a monstrous, huge place filled with strangers. He shuddered.

"Ian Dare?" A waiter strode up to Ian with his packaged order.

"Thanks," Ian said, accepting the bag.

"You can pay up front."

Ian nodded and turned back to Alex. "I've said enough already. I guess I should just leave you with what Riley told me. If you're really invested in Madison, you're going to have to be patient and dig in for the long haul."

Alex tipped his head in acknowledgment. "Hey, man. Thanks."

Ian gave him a grim smile.

An awkward silence ensued. "Guess I better get my wife her food."

"Congratulations. Sorry I didn't mention it earlier. Guess I'm still working on the self-absorbed thing."

Ian grinned. "I hear it's part of your charm."

"Asshole," Alex muttered.

With a laugh, Ian walked away, leaving Alex alone with his newfound unsettling knowledge about Madison.

*   *   *

Madison arrived at her foster mother's house early Sunday morning, intending to help her move to the nursing home a few short miles away. In her possession, she had the documents permitting her to take Franny with her in case Eric arrived to cause an argument. She hoped he wouldn't, as upheaval and loud noises only upset his mother. But it would be good for Franny to have her son by her side when she entered someplace brand new.

She decided to spend some time with Franny and see what kind of day today was before putting her in the car. In the meantime, her aide would pack up the car.

"Franny?" Madison walked into the kitchen.

Franny sat dressed, staring out the window behind the table. She turned and looked at Madison. "Gracie, what took you so long to get here?"

Madison sighed. Gracie was Franny's sister who'd passed away five years earlier. "I hit a little traffic," she said, knowing it was easier to keep Franny settled and calm than upset her with what she didn't remember.

"We're going to take you to your new home today."

Franny didn't answer.

Madison settled into a chair beside her. The other woman's hair, brown streaked with some gray, had been brushed and her clothes chosen by the aide. Madison worried Franny would miss Linda once she was in the home, before reminding herself Franny likely wouldn't remember the aide soon anyway.

"The walls are pale blue, like your room is now. You said that's one of the reasons you chose the place."

"I love blue. It's my favorite color. It was Daniel's too," Franny said, and Madison realized she had her foster mom with her again.

"Everything you're used to having around you, the pictures, and mementos, they're all coming with you."

She patted Madison's hand. "You're so good to me."

Madison swallowed hard. "You've been good to me too." She smiled.

"Are we ready? I don't want to spend any more time here wishing I didn't have to leave," Franny said.

Madison stood and held out her hand. Franny placed her smaller weathered hand inside hers, and they walked out to the car.

Eric never showed up, which left the burden of the transition entirely on Madison. But her home aide had already packed up Franny's most important possessions and necessities, and once Madison brought her to the car, the trip went easily.

Getting Franny settled didn't go as smoothly. Once they entered the new surroundings, Franny became argumentative and belligerent. It wasn't something that happened often, but her aide had reported it was occurring more lately. It had led them to push ahead with the move sooner rather than later. Madison hoped the older woman would settle in with her new caretakers easily once she left.

After meeting with the director, she returned to Franny's room to find her foster mom ranting and yelling at her new nurse, who'd delivered her dinner on a tray.

"Franny, this is Sharon, remember? You met her when we arrived."

"Get out!" Franny yelled.

Madison stepped closer. "Listen—"

"It's your fault I'm in here. I hate you," Franny yelled, grabbing the food tray and throwing it at Madison.

She ducked, and the nurse grasped her arm, leading her out of the room.

Shaking, hurt, and upset, Madison leaned against the wall in the hallway.

"I'm sorry," Sharon, the middle-aged nurse, said. "This often happens more during the adjustment period. Give it some time, and she'll settle in.

Madison swallowed hard. "I hope so. Please call if you need me."

"We will." Sharon patted her on the shoulder.

Madison left the home, depression surrounding her like a shroud. She climbed into her car and started the motor, resting her head on the steering wheel before starting her drive.

If she were smart, she'd drive home and go straight to bed. But she needed a shoulder to cry on. Riley was pregnant and sick, busy with her new husband and life. She'd promised herself she wouldn't rely on Alex, but his shoulder was the only one she wanted.

And he was the only person she had in her life who she could imagine turning to.

FIVE

Alex hit the gym on the top floor of his building. He might not play football any longer, but he refused to let himself get soft. Ian gave him access to the gym at the stadium, but working out with the Thunder players still felt like being surrounded by the opposition. It helped in his new job that he practiced what he preached, but he kept fit for himself. He finished his workout and wiped the sweat from his face with a towel.

After gathering his things, he checked his phone and saw a number he didn't recognize. Whoever it was had left a message. He waited for the elevator and hit play.

"Hi, Alex. It's Rachel Bradley." His college girlfriend.

The one he'd thought he'd been in love with. Before she'd hurt him badly. "I know it's been a while, but I have something to discuss with you. I think you'll find it worth your while to call me back." He ended the message without waiting for more, memories of his time with Rachel coming back to him.

They'd hooked up early on at UF, and they'd stayed together for four years. He'd thought they had a future. She'd never had any intention of marrying a football player or living a life that involved long stretches out of town and female fans flocking around him. Of course it would've been nice if she'd told him that at any point during their time together when he'd brought up the future. She hadn't. But she had broken up with him after graduation.

The Rachel he remembered hadn't been a mean girl. She hadn't used people to her advantage. She'd just never worked up the courage to tell him he wanted more than she did. And he'd felt like an ass for exposing his heart to someone who hadn't wanted it at all.

He shook his head, not even curious about why she'd be calling him now. She'd done enough damage and taught him the one solid lesson he'd kept with him ever since, setting the stage for the non-relationships that had come after her. Since Rachel, he'd never been tempted to let anyone in.

Until Madison.

He shook his head, knowing revisiting the past would only work him into a frustrated state. He'd grown up enough, been through enough women to trust that Madison wasn't the type to hide her feelings from him. She said what she meant and meant what she said. He understood who she was and why. He was going out of his comfort zone to pursue her despite knowing how heavily she was trying to resist him. He didn't need messages from Rachel screwing with his head, he thought, and hit delete on the call.

He took the elevator to his apartment, surprised to find Madison leaning against his door.

"Madison?"

She raised tear-filled eyes to his.

"Hey." He held out his arms, and she stepped inside his embrace.

He had no idea what had brought her here and hated seeing her upset, but the fact that she'd come to him opened up a world of hope he hadn't been feeling. He was sweaty, and he probably smelled from his workout, but she didn't seem to mind as she burrowed in close, her head against his chest.

His heart ached as he held her, telling him these feelings he had for her were only getting stronger. That he wanted to ride them out and not run said a lot for the changes that damned injury had wrought. He wrapped her into him and let her release whatever she'd bottled up inside until eventually her quiet sniffling eased.

"Come inside," he said, letting them into the

apartment.

She nodded. "I'm sorry to just show up and then fall apart like this."

"It's not a problem." He locked the door behind them and tossed his keys onto the nearest counter.

She followed him into the kitchen, where he grabbed a cold bottle of vitamin water from the fridge. "Iced tea?" he asked, gesturing to the bottled brand she liked.

She nodded and he poured her a glass.

"Want to talk about it?" he asked.

"I took Franny to the nursing home today. I helped her home aide move her out of the home she's lived in most of her life and into a strange place she picked out but didn't recognize." She swiped at her damp eyes.

"She was angry and mean, which is something that's been happening more often lately. The doctor says it's part of the disease but…" She paused, obviously pulling herself together. "I don't know what's worse. When she doesn't remember me at all or when she's throwing things and saying she hates me."

Oh shit. He grasped her hand. "I'm sorry."

She forced a smile. "Yeah. Me too."

"Did your foster brother help?" he asked.

She shook her head. "He did leave me a loving phone message I got while I was waiting here. He said since it was my decision, I could deal with it and live with the consequences. The bastard."

"That kind of behavior should help you in court."

"I hope so. I just don't know."

She looked so defeated he didn't know what to do to make it better.

"I appreciate you listening, but I should go. You probably want to shower, and I'm just in the way." She rose to her feet.

He jumped up, determined to keep her here. "Did you eat dinner?" he asked.

She shook her head.

"Lunch?" he asked, because she'd been busy taking care of her foster mom and not herself.

"No."

He frowned, but he wasn't surprised. "That settles it. I'll order us dinner and I'll jump in the shower. Okay?"

Madison nodded. "I'd like that," she said softly.

"Make yourself comfortable. I'll be quick."

She settled into the oversized couch, the one thing along with the massive television he'd moved from his old house. "Remote's on the table," he said before heading for the bedroom.

He showered quickly, wanting to get back to her as soon as possible. Madison was here, and he recognized she was at her most vulnerable. A turning point if there ever was one. He wouldn't take advantage, but he would be there for her and make damned sure she knew she was no longer alone.

* * *

Madison rubbed her bare arms and cuddled farther into the soft velour cushions on Alex's couch. She didn't turn on the television because this was the first minute of downtime she'd had all day, and she wanted to just *be*. And savor the fact that, for the moment at least, she wasn't dealing with life by herself. It felt so good to not be alone, she thought, closing her eyes and letting go.

She had no idea how much time had passed when the couch dipped with heavy weight.

"Hey," Alex said in that sexy deep voice.

She looked up at him and smiled. "Hey."

He wore nylon sweats, no shirt, and he smelled so good she wanted to crawl beneath his skin. She had no defenses left today to fight the attraction. She didn't want to.

"Feeling a little better?" he asked, stroking her cheek with one finger.

"Yeah."

"I'm glad you came to me."

She smiled. "I'm glad I had somewhere *to* go."

"Madison—"

The doorbell rang, interrupting him. "That's dinner. I'll get it," he said.

A few minutes later they were sitting at his table eating Emilio's pasta. To her surprise, she was feeling not only better but hungry.

She didn't want to focus on her own life and problems, and he seemed to understand. They talked about work and Riley's pregnancy and laughed over the fact that Ian was running to feed her pregnancy cravings.

"Are things really better between you and Ian?" she asked, hoping he didn't mind talking about their relationship.

In the past, he'd always deflected questions about himself, causing her to do the same. She knew it was his way of keeping a distance between them, and the few times he'd slipped and revealed something intimate, he'd immediately rebuilt his walls. She didn't really think she'd get far now, but she wanted to know and decided to ask. Besides, better to shine the spotlight on his family rather than her lack thereof.

"When I ran into him the other night at the restaurant, he seemed ... more interested in my life. Of course it could be so he can have a few laughs at my expense. I'm never sure."

She chuckled at his supposition. "From what I've seen, Ian is a man of few words. The ones he uses, he tends to mean. If he asks, he's interested."

He raised an eyebrow. "You think so?" He paused in thought. "You're probably right. I'm interested in him. I always was. I guess that's why it bothered me so much that he didn't feel the same way. But I get why now."

They'd finished dinner, and she pushed her plate aside, more interested in what he was revealing than cleaning up. Alex was actually confiding in her, and she was mesmerized by every word.

"The thing is, I didn't have it bad growing up," Alex continued. "I mean, I wasn't stupid. I knew something was off between my mother and father. He lived with us, but my parents weren't married, and we didn't have Dad's last name. That's unusual by any standards."

"Did you know why they weren't married?"

He shook his head. "As I got older, it only took a few strokes of the keyboard to find out all I needed to know about Robert Dare, hotel magnate."

"Ouch," Madison said softly.

He shrugged, obviously not all that upset by the memory. "It was weird. It didn't hurt as much as it should have, I guess because I knew we had a father who was always there."

"Did you confront him?" she asked.

He nodded. "I stormed into their bedroom one night and demanded answers. It turns out Mom knew he had another family all along. He explained how it was complicated and I'd understand more when I was older, but basically his marriage was one of convenience only." He shook his head. "Clearly more than that since they had kids, but at the time, I didn't give much thought to it. I mean, I was only fifteen when I figured it all out."

"Then Sienna got sick?" Madison asked, knowing those touchy details from Riley.

"Childhood leukemia." He visibly shuddered. "My baby sister, deathly ill. We thought we'd lose her. I mean, my mother actually prepared us, using those words. And one look at Sienna in the hospital, on the rare times we were allowed in to visit her ... it was obvious why they were so scared." His voiced came out gruff and affected.

Unable to stop herself, she rose and walked over to him, intending to give him a comforting hug. He pulled her down onto his lap, obviously wanting the intimate connection. After the day she'd had, she needed the same thing.

"What happened?" she asked.

"Dad had no choice but to go to his wife—Ian's mother—and ask her to have his other children's bone marrow tested."

"Wow. That's like a soap opera."

"Yet disturbingly real. I think that's when it hit

home for everyone. Dad had another wife and family, who, as it turned out, knew nothing about my mother or his other kids. It taught us all that my father is definitely a selfish son of a bitch."

She lay her head against his chest, listening to his rapidly beating heart.

"I lied. When I said the stuff about my father and us not having his name didn't bother me? It did. I just hated to think about why we were different. What it could mean."

"I never liked thinking about my parents at all," she murmured.

"Anything you want to talk about now?" he asked.

She shook her head.

"So tonight's about me baring my soul?"

She grinned, knowing he couldn't see. "It's about time, don't you think?"

His low chuckle reverberated through her, but she had no doubt she'd have to return the favor one day soon.

"Well, on the one hand, I was grateful I had a father who was present. On the other ... kids can be brutal."

"They made fun of you?" she asked, horrified on his behalf. Although she wasn't surprised. She'd experienced her own fair share of being made fun of for her hand-me-down clothes and *fake* families.

"They only called us bastards once. I was big enough to hold my own, and so was Jason. Nobody bothered us after we made our point the first time. It was easy to defend my position. As a kid, I trusted in what I'd been told, that my parents didn't believe in the institution of marriage." He idly stroked her hair, and she sighed in contentment.

"And now?" she asked, ever perceptive.

"As I got older, I recognized the damage my father had caused. It was harder for Ian than for me."

"From what Riley told me, Ian idolized your father. His disillusion was the hardest."

Alex nodded. "All the time Dad was with us, Ian and his four siblings thought he was traveling on business. It made sense since he had hotels all over the country, and they were used to him being an absentee parent. Then he showed up asking for bone marrow for a kid they knew nothing about, only to find out there was another woman and two other children."

Was it any wonder he'd ended up bitter and angry about relationships? Madison mused. "Yet despite it all, Ian's mother allowed her kids to be tested. That's pretty amazing."

"I agree. And as icing on an already sucky cake, Dad decided, since everything was out in the open, it was time to officially ask for a divorce. He married my mother as soon as it was final." Alex groaned. "It's like the shit you see on reality TV. And it's no wonder Ian resented us. He became the glue that held his mother and siblings together, and we got the father we always had anyway, along with his name."

"None of that is your fault," she assured him.

"Maybe not, but I was too thick-headed to get it. I thought I'd gained this hotshot sibling who was going to University of Florida to play football. I wanted to follow in his footsteps. Be like him."

"And he wanted nothing to do with you."

"And things went to hell between us from there," Alex said, admitting all this for the first time, out loud and to himself.

"I bet it hurt," Madison said, tilting her head up at him. She looked into his deep dark eyes, the handsome face showing all the confusion and pain he kept hidden.

That he was revealing it to her now eased the ever-present constriction in her chest.

"Yeah. And as you know, I don't react well when hurt, physically or emotionally." He slid his thumb over her bottom lip.

She licked at his salty finger, doing her best not to moan at the intimate contact.

He cleared his throat. "Anyway, that's when my official rivalry with Ian began."

"And it took Riley to end it," she concluded, and

he nodded.

"Can I ask you something?" She glanced away from him as she spoke.

He cocked his head to one side and grinned. "Might as well. I seem to be in an answering mood."

She refused to meet his gaze. "Do you ... or did you have feelings for Riley beyond friendship? Is that why you gave her such a hard time when she met Ian? Because you wanted her for yourself?"

She asked the one question that had always haunted her, even when she knew that, to Riley, there had never been more than sisterly feelings for Alex.

He lifted her chin, forcing her to look into his eyes and face both him and her question, which was all too revealing.

"No, I am not interested in Riley that way. But in the interest of full disclosure, I can't say that I didn't try to hook up with her once."

Madison's stomach plummeted at the admission, but she'd asked. She had to accept the answer.

"What can I say? I'm a guy, and we do have our idiot moments." He chuckled, obviously trying to lighten the moment.

Madison didn't laugh with him.

He grasped her face in his hands. "There is nothing between me and Riley but a lifelong friendship. She's like my sister. I saved her from a bad situation when we were kids, and it bonded us even more, but that's it. There's only one woman I'm interested in now," he said, his tone gruff.

He removed his thumb and closed his lips over hers, sliding back and forth, coaxing her to open. He didn't have to try hard. Her defenses were low, her need high. This was Alex, and she'd wanted him for so long. Even when he'd been gone from her life and she should have hated him, she'd still desired him. And now she was going to have him, she thought, parting her lips and letting him in.

Alex realized that in answering Madison's questions, he had received answers too, and he decided it was time. She was ready to resume a relationship. Not where they'd left off but somewhere fresh and new. This desire consuming not just his body but his emotions was definitely new to him. Acknowledging it and not running, newer still.

"Up," he said, deciding to take over.

She stood.

He rose and grasped her hand, pulling her toward the couch, where she lay down, enabling him to stretch out beside her. He looked into her eyes and tucked her hair behind her ear, the moment as intimate as any in his life.

She leaned into him, and he glided his tongue along the seam of her lips. Dipped his fingers into her hair, tilting her head in the exact position he needed for complete control. He slid his hand down her side, grasped the bottom of her shirt, and pulled it up and over her head. He clamped her wrists in one hand, holding her in place, then pinned her lower body against the couch with his hips. His cock found a home in the cradle of her thighs, his erection hard and aching but exactly where he wanted to be.

"I need to fuck you, Angel," he said, his low, gravelly voice revealing the depths of his hunger and desire for her. "I need to be so deep I don't know where you end and I begin."

Her eyes glazed at his words. "So do it."

His body shuddered at her sweet acquiescence. He kissed her lips, grazed her neck with his mouth, his teeth. Worked his way lower, nibbling on her soft skin, her collarbone, until she was soft and pliable beneath him. He continued, stretching the cup of her bra beneath her breast. Gripping her arm tighter, he pulled the already taut nipple into his mouth, suckling hard.

With a groan, she tried to free her hands, but he held fast. Her whimper told him how much she needed him. Her hips bucked against his. Sliding deep inside her now would be too easy. It would give her the release she sought, but it wouldn't prove to her that she needed *him*.

He spent more time on her breasts, divesting her

of her lace bra so he could mold and cup the soft mounds of flesh in his hands while tormenting her nipples with his tongue and teeth. Hands freed, she gripped his head, pulling at his hair, begging him to stop, to keep going, her need so intense, just as he'd planned.

She had sensitive breasts, and he loved making a feast out of them, knowing she was out of her mind with the same desire throbbing hard and heavy in his veins.

"Alex, please." Her hips gyrated beneath his, taking his cock along for the ride.

"Tell me what you want," he said through clenched teeth, because holding back was costing him too.

Glazed blue eyes stared back at him. Eyes he'd seen in his dreams, that had gotten him through his nightmares. He didn't realize how much he'd relied on the memory of her until now.

Soon she would be so much more than a memory, he thought, ready to possess her in every way possible.

SIX

Madison's body pulsed with yearning, and desire flooded every part of her being. Her nipples were sensitive from his sensual torment, which seemed to never end. Every lick, nip, and touch sent a shot of awareness to her core. She pulled on his silky hair, begging without words for him to fill her, and when that didn't work, she pleaded out loud. But he held back, ignoring her throbbing sex in favor of arousing her to the point of pain.

He raised himself up.

Madison had never been more aware of the strength Alex possessed than now with his hard, gorgeous body stretched over hers. Tattoos, which he'd freely admitted to getting for juvenile kicks, covered his forearms and broad shoulders, and muscles bunched in his biceps. Yet he held himself in check. Why?

And wasn't that the loaded question.

He shifted his hips, his hard erection sliding

against her clit through her shorts. She needed relief, but he was withholding hers, as well as his own.

"Tell me, Angel. What do you want?" His gruff voice added to the awareness ricocheting between them.

"You," she said, nearly breathless. "I want you."

He suddenly rolled off of her and stood, shoving his sweatpants down and off. She managed to get rid of her shorts and panties just as quickly. Next thing she knew, he'd lifted her up and started walking toward the bedroom.

She shrieked and wrapped her arms around him, aware of his hard male body as she cuddled close. "What are you doing?"

"Taking you to bed."

"I like the sound of that." She kissed his jaw and nibbled on his earlobe, nipping lightly right before he laid her down on the big mattress.

"Lots of room to maneuver," he said with a grin.

He returned, his thick erection sliding directly over her damp pussy, and she moaned at the intimate contact.

"Feel good?" he asked, holding his thick cock with one hand and rubbing over and over her clit.

"So, so good." Beautiful waves washed through her, and she arched, needing more pressure. Needing him.

He glided harder against her, knowing the rhythm and level of contact she needed. He hadn't forgotten. Knew exactly what would make her come. His erection was thick and hard and bringing her higher. The peak tempted her, building swells teased her, and suddenly what had been out of reach crashed over her as Alex took her over the edge.

"Yes, Alex, yes," she moaned loudly.

She was quivering with aftershocks when he thrust into her. "That's right, Angel, it's me."

She was slick from her orgasm, ready for him, and she accepted him easily. He filled the empty ache, but what scared her more was the wash of sensation that accompanied his glide inside of her. He drew out and pushed back in farther this time, stopping when he was buried all the way. She clenched her inner walls around him, holding him in tightly.

"You feel so good. Hot and slick." He shifted his hips, and she sighed in pure delight. "I want you to come again, and this time, scream my name."

She arched up, pulling him impossibly deeper. "Hurry, please."

His dark gaze locked on hers. "My pleasure," he muttered and began to plunge into her with all the need and desire pounding through her veins.

"Yes, yes," she moaned in time with his thrusts. In and out, he urged her toward nirvana. Every shift and undulation of their hips brought her higher.

Their bodies, slick and overheated, came together hard. He kissed her, his tongue mimicking the act of their bodies as he devoured her everywhere. With each determined plunge in, his pelvis ground against her sex, taking her ever up, higher and closer to climax.

"Oh, Alex." She extended his name on a low shuddering moan.

"Yes, Angel. You're almost there."

"I am." Her entire being trembled with the relentless friction of their bodies. She grabbed his shoulders, digging her nails in deep and arching her lower half upward.

He picked up his rhythm, and the second he moved again, the tremors started in earnest. "Alex, yes, yes, yes!" she cried out as her world exploded, and he came inside her, long hot spurts she felt everywhere.

He collapsed on top of her, his breathing ragged, his big body warm and heavy. The reality of what she'd done quickly washed over her, but she couldn't regret something so wonderful. So instead, she let herself enjoy the great sex, the phenomenal orgasms, and the man who'd given them to her.

She let out a satisfied sigh.

Alex propped himself up on one arm and stared into her eyes, unnerving her with the intensity. But after what they'd shared, she felt the same way.

"Are you okay?" he asked.

"Never better," she said. "That was amazing."

His sexy grin said he agreed.

"So when can we do it again?" Just looking at him and she wanted to climb back into his arms.

"First things first." He cleared his throat. "We didn't use protection. I should have grabbed a condom but—"

She blew out a long breath. "I'm still on the pill." But they'd been careless, and she knew it.

He let out a relieved breath. "Okay. And I haven't been with anyone since you."

Which, if she believed him, meant he was serious about her. She shook off the thought, unwilling to go there. This was fun, and she intended to enjoy it. As many times as she could.

"You're quiet."

"Just thinking."

"I'm serious. I told you I've changed. That hit to the head was an eye opener." He cupped her jaw in his hand. "Not to mention, I couldn't get you out of my head."

She swallowed hard, his words obviously getting to her. "Really?"

He leaned in close and brushed his lips over hers. "Yeah. Now do you still want to do it again?"

She laughed and crawled on top of him, straddling

him with her naked body. No small talk, just enjoyment.

That she could handle.

He gripped her ass and grinned. "Condoms in the drawer. Grab one and ride me," he said, his eyes dark with desire.

She found protection and took her time sheathing him, covering his silken erection with the condom before she straddled him, lowering herself inch by long, thick inch. Then she did as he instructed and began to move.

Alex had to force his eyes open, to watch the expressions on Madison's face and not concentrate solely on her slick walls enclosing him in heat. Better than he remembered. He now knew why he hadn't been able to bring himself to call any other woman. Nobody had ever felt like this. And now that he wasn't fighting the feelings, sensation and something more overwhelmed him.

It took everything in him to remain in place, not flip her over and take her hard and fast this time. But she was milking his cock and, from the sublime look on her face, enjoying every minute. She looked gorgeous astride him, head tilted, lips parted, her hair falling down her back.

He gripped her thighs, and she moaned, raising her head, meeting his gaze, her pupils dilated.

"Flip us?" she asked.

He grinned. "Gladly."

He pulled out of her and stood, sliding her to the edge of the bed. "Umm, not sure this is what I had in mind," she said in a husky voice.

"I want to be deeper in that hot pussy, Angel." He raised her legs over his shoulders, and her eyes opened wide.

Before she could react, he thrust back inside her only to pull out again.

She groaned, and he laughed, tunneling back in slowly, making her squirm and arch her hips in an attempt to pull him all the way. "I'm going to make you pay for this, you know."

"I certainly hope so."

She narrowed her gaze, and he took her completely, thrusting deep and hard, so his balls slapped against her ass and his eyes rolled back in his head. Then it was too late to tease her any more because his body demanded release.

Short strokes followed longer ones. Madison panted and moaned, clasping her tight sheath around his cock with every thrust and grind of his hips. He slipped his hand between them, pressing hard on her clit, and as her tremors began, he let himself go, losing himself inside her.

Long after Madison left, he lay awake, running the

night over in his head. One thing was clear. This woman owned him, and she had no damned clue.

* * *

Another week of work almost over, Madison thought. Another week of nonstop attention from Alex. He picked up coffee, brought her lunch, walked her to her car, and basically acted like the most attentive man ever. Her new relationship with him helped her put the situation with her foster brother out of her mind until her next meeting with the lawyer and the upcoming hearing.

In the meantime, work also kept her busy.

She glanced over at Alex. Feet propped up on his desk, he hung up the phone as his gaze landed on hers. And darkened. "What's up, Angel?"

"I'm leaving for the meeting with the head of the PR team Ian recommended. Are you sure you don't want to join me?" she asked.

"I'll leave PR to you. I'm meeting my sister for dinner. Are you sure you don't want to cancel your plans and come along?"

She laughed. "Work, Alex. Work has to come first."

"You know what they say about all work and no play," he said in an attempt to tease her.

She rolled her eyes as she grabbed her purse from

her drawer. "You play plenty." He'd talked her into letting him stay over at her place, which meant they'd *played* last night and again in the shower this morning.

"I didn't hear you complaining either." He swung his feet onto the floor, rose, and strode over, intent and desire written all over his expressive face.

"Uh-uh. I have to go. We have a meeting in the morning with the PR team and all the department heads. I want to make sure I know exactly what he's going to pitch. I don't want to be caught off guard."

He braced an arm on the back of her chair and tilted her head up toward his. "Will I see you after your dinner?"

"If you're lucky."

He pressed his lips to hers before beginning to lick a path toward the sweet spot behind her ear. "What do I have to do to get lucky?" he asked.

Her nipples puckered into tight buds, and she squirmed in her seat. "Be good." She gripped the arms of her chair.

"I'm always good."

He was good, she thought. So, so good.

He slid a hand onto her thigh, immediately sliding upward beneath her skirt.

"Alex, no. I have a meeting."

"And I want you thinking of me the whole time." He brushed his fingertips over her panties, unerringly finding her clit, and she swallowed a moan.

"Mission accomplished," she murmured, knowing she'd be wet and wanting Alex the entire time. "But we're not doing this here."

To her surprise, he immediately eased his hand out and sat back against the desk. "If you insist." A teasing glint lit his gaze.

He knew he'd lit her fuse and left her burning. "Come to my place after," he said.

"We'll see what time I get out." She didn't want to make any promises, no matter how much she wanted to be with him again. She really should go home for the night, sleep alone in her bed once in a while, and not learn to rely on how good it felt to be with him.

"Where are you going for dinner?" he asked.

She looked up, her gaze falling on the vee in his button-down shirt, where his oh-so-lickable chest was exposed, and she sighed.

"Emilio's," she said. Derek Fine, head of the PR company, had asked her where she'd like to meet, and the restaurant near Alex's apartment had just popped out of her mouth.

He grinned. "Well, it just so happens that I'm meeting my sister there too. No excuses then."

She shook her head and laughed at how easy she'd made it. Of course, she wondered if that had been the point all along. "I guess I'll see you a little later."

His answer was a long, lingering kiss. One she couldn't resist, and she threaded her fingers into his silky hair and kissed him back.

The ringing of his cell interrupted the moment, and he stepped back, regret on his face.

"Get it," she said. "I have to leave anyway."

He walked over and grabbed his phone from the desk. He glanced at the number, and his expression turned downright chilly before he hit a button and shoved the cell into his back pocket.

"Who was it?" she asked.

His eyes grew shuttered. "No one important."

Which meant just the opposite or his entire mood wouldn't have shifted.

She admitted to being curious, but she wouldn't pry, and she had a business dinner, and she needed to get moving.

"See you later," she murmured.

"Yeah." He stared out the window, not looking her way.

He was suddenly distant and distracted, confirming her suspicion that *no one important* was emphatically significant. And Alex was keeping the *who* to himself.

*   *   *

Alex stared at the dull office ceiling long after Madison walked out. This was the third time Rachel had called.

What the hell did she want after all this time? He couldn't help wondering. Despite his insistence that he didn't care, he couldn't deny that her calls and the corresponding return of memories along with them had left him shaken.

He'd reached his car when his sister called to say a professor had assigned a last-minute paper and she needed to cancel their dinner plans.

Although Alex had neglected his family for too long, his new job, his new woman, and the feeling of doing something important for the first time in ages had him wanting to fix other areas of his life too. So he'd reached out to Sienna, but he understood her reasons for rescheduling.

In truth, he was relieved. He needed time to deal with the anger and frustration Rachel's calls brought up inside him. So the woman he'd naively thought he'd marry had dumped him after graduation. He'd done damn well without her. Rachel was a distant memory. But the hurt of rejection wasn't.

Rejection and the feeling of not being good enough hadn't been new to him when Rachel had dumped him. There'd been Ian, the half brother who'd wanted nothing to do with him. Alex had found out about Ian when he was fifteen. He'd Googled him, learned all they had in common, and idolized him, wanting to be just like him. Wanting an older brother who understood him. But Ian hadn't wanted a damn thing to do with Alex, not as kids and not as adults. Not until Ian had wanted Riley, who'd come with Alex as part of her self-built family, did he agree to get to know Alex.

He hadn't been good enough on his own. That was the underlying message. One Rachel had reinforced when she'd left. And one that had sacked him again when his injury had sidelined him from pro football permanently.

Although it had been a while since he'd indulged in self-pity, Rachel's calls brought up a whole host of shit, and he felt the need for a drink and some time alone.

*   *   *

Madison arrived at work the next morning in time to head directly to the meeting. She didn't want to go to her office and deal with Alex when she needed to be focused on the PR campaign about to be proposed. It was edgy and spot-on and, in her mind, brilliant. She hoped everyone involved would go for the concept. Especially Alex.

If she'd seen him last night, she'd have run the idea past him. If he'd called and explained his no-show at the restaurant, she'd have told him they needed to talk. Instead, after convincing her to spend the night at his place, he'd changed plans and gone MIA. Between his mood swing after the unanswered phone call and his silence afterward, she let her insecurities hold sway and decided *not* to reach out first.

She strode into the room wearing the suit she felt the most powerful and comfortable in. Did it help that the cream color accentuated her lightly tanned skin and that, even with a camisole that appropriately covered her breasts, she felt both feminine and sexy? Of course. Because she had a feeling she'd need all the armor she could get.

"Madison!"

She turned at the sound of Riley calling her name. "Hi!" She hugged her friend, then pulled back to look her over. "You look fantastic. So much better than last time I saw you."

Riley grinned. "That's because I'm not nauseous anymore, so I'm not green around the gills. And the cravings have started, not to mention, I'm eating for two." She laughed. "My curves are back and then some."

"But you're happy and I'm so glad."

"I really am. Are you?"

Before Madison could answer, Ian strode into the room, and the atmosphere changed from people chattering to silence. The man commanded respect, that was for sure.

Except from his wife, who rolled her eyes and pinned Madison with an intense stare. "I'm waiting for an answer."

"I'm fine." She gripped her folders tighter in her hand. "I should go sit," she murmured.

Alex hadn't arrived, and she chose a chair in the conference room next to Derek Fine, the head of the Fine PR Firm, with whom she'd had dinner last night. Riley sat beside her, obviously intending to continue her inquisition.

The room began to fill up. Alex walked in last, wearing black slacks and a white button-down shirt. Unlike Ian, he eschewed a tie, but he was every inch professional—except he looked as if he hadn't slept, his eyes bloodshot and his mouth drawn tight. Something was wrong. She just had no idea what. And her gut told her things were about to get even dicier.

"Madison, are you ready to begin?" Ian asked from the head of the table.

She nodded. Hands folded in front of her, she spoke. "In addition to the program we intend to institute, Ian has spoken of taking this campaign nationwide. With the right angle, we can protect the players and institute more safety measures than exist so far. We can also encourage all teams in all contact sports to educate their players for the future. To further this endeavor, the Fine PR Firm has a presentation for us to consider. I've seen the concept, and it's brave and edgy," she said, not meeting Alex's steady gaze, although she felt his focus as if it were a tangible touch.

Whatever had triggered his mood last night, she needed to be at her best right now. Her personal life would have to wait.

*   *   *

Alex watched Madison with pride as she addressed the people in the room. She was masterful, holding everyone's attention. And he was such an ass, to have ignored her in favor of whiskey last night and a hangover this morning.

At the time, he'd thought he'd had his reasons for needing time alone. This morning, he regretted his selfish actions. He was well aware that Madison was still waiting for him to screw up in some way. And he had. Royally.

She wouldn't look at him, not that he blamed her. And though he'd gotten here early enough to talk to her in their office, it had never dawned on him that she'd avoid him there and come straight to the conference room instead. He had to give her credit, she was impressive in anything she did, and as she primed the room for whatever was to come, he couldn't tear his gaze away.

A cream-colored suit with a deep vee and matching camisole drew his attention to her full breasts. Though they were well covered, he knew exactly what those mounds looked like, how her nipples puckered when aroused, and the jacket molded perfectly to her curves. Her blue eyes flashed with passion as she spoke. Because he'd been the recipient of that fire firsthand, watching her now aroused his baser instincts, making him itch to haul her into their private office and grovel. On his knees, hands sliding beneath her skirt and begging her forgiveness in the one way he knew she couldn't resist.

"And so I'd like to introduce Derek Fine," Madison said, and applause broke out around the table, drawing Alex's attention to more appropriate subjects. But that didn't stop his body from pulsing with need.

The man she'd introduced rose and walked to the front of the room. One of his associates dimmed the lights, and Fine gestured to the wall on which now flashed a PowerPoint presentation. With his mouth like cotton and his head pounding, Alex knew he wasn't paying nearly enough attention, but he'd just have to catch up later. He covered a yawn and tried harder to focus.

"The idea is to bring focus and attention to the problem, and who better than the man who is spearheading the effort? We suggest a national campaign at football stadiums, bus stops, and television spots. Like this."

Alex stared in shock as his prone body flashed across the wall seconds after his career-ending hit. Each successive screen, in time to the sound of a camera shutter click, showed the succession of what had happened next, from coaches bending over him to paramedics arriving to the ultimate humiliation, his body on the stretcher, neck stabilizer holding his head in place as he was carried off the field for the final time. The words PROTECT, EDUCATE, and SUCCEED flashed beneath, ending with Alex in a suit and tie, the Thunder Dome superimposed behind him.

"What the fuck?" He swung his head away from the presentation to Madison, who thankfully had decided to look his way.

She stared back at him, unwavering. "It's brilliant, Alex. Overcoming tragedy with triumph. You'd be showing all players what's possible."

"No way. I took this as a behind-the-scenes job. I'm not going to be the goddamned poster boy for the campaign so the rest of the league can view me as weak."

"That's not the plan," Madison said patiently.

As if he were the freaking idiot they'd just showed on the screen. "I said no. It's not happening." He rose to his feet, the mild headache he'd nursed all morning suddenly full-blown. "I should've been consulted before this shit was presented," he muttered and started for the door.

"Alex—" Ian rose to block his way.

"Step aside," he warned his half brother.

Ian met his gaze. He must have seen something in Alex's expression that had him moving away from the door. "This discussion isn't over," he said under his breath.

"The hell it isn't." Alex stormed out of the room and headed for his office, where he could grab his car keys and get the hell out of here.

*   *   *

Madison watched Alex storm out of the room in complete and utter shock. When she'd gauged his reaction ahead of time, she'd thought maybe he'd balk. Argue. Offer resistance until they explained why this was such a good idea. Instead, he'd marched out without discussion.

She turned back to the table and met Ian's gaze.

"Ri? You want to talk to him?" He probably figured as Alex's closest friend, Riley was the obvious choice to deal with him in his furious state.

Not happening, Madison thought, jumping up from her seat. "I'll go." If anyone was going to talk to him, it was Madison.

They had more to resolve between them than just the issue of the PR campaign ... and she was feeling a bit territorial at the moment.

Riley nodded at her, a slight grin on her face.

"Can you handle Derek Fine?" she asked, ignoring her friend and approaching Ian instead.

He nodded. "I like the proposal, but I get where he's coming from," Ian said, surprising her.

She narrowed her gaze. "I thought he might be surprised, maybe have to be talked into it, but I didn't anticipate such anger." She was still shaken by his reaction.

"You didn't see him after he was told he couldn't play anymore," Riley said, coming up beside them. "I mean, I know you did, but not the fallout after." Riley touched Madison's shoulder. "Go talk to him. He'll listen to you."

With a nod, Madison headed out.

She reached their office in time to catch him in the hall, car keys in hand. "We need to talk," she said before he could speak first.

He shook his head, every muscle in his body tight. "Not now. I need to cool off first."

Now she was the one who was annoyed. "I thought you did that last night." She pinned him with an angry stare of her own.

She remembered the last time he'd been hurting

and angry. He'd thrown her out of his room and his life, and she'd let him. This time, she would be proactive, and she intended to have her say.

"Fine." He turned toward their office and strode inside. He walked to the small window and looked out before turning toward her. "I was an ass last night, and I'm sorry."

She'd been ready for a fight. Instead she'd received an apology? "What?"

"You heard me." He shoved his hands into his pockets. "I was planning to talk to you this morning, but you weren't here. Then I was blindsided by the proposal—"

"You wouldn't have been if I'd either seen you last night as planned or if you'd called to tell me you needed a night alone." She folded her arms across her chest, self-protection at its finest, she thought.

"I realize that *now*. At the time, I needed time alone."

Hurt flooded every inch of her being. "Well, it's not like I was the one who practically seduced you into agreeing to spend the night together. That was all you." It was important to her that he knew she didn't need him. That he'd been the one pushing for more time together. She'd never be the woman who wanted too much from him. Or from anyone.

"I know."

"Well, it would have been nice if you'd informed me that you'd changed your mind. Or that you needed space." She hated the hurt in her voice, the power any show of emotion gave him over her, but she couldn't control her feelings from escaping.

"I didn't need space from you, Angel."

"Right. That's why you didn't call." She shook her head. "I was there, remember? You got a phone call, your mood changed, and suddenly the sexy, teasing Alex was replaced by some ice-cold version who just walked out. You didn't think I'd notice the change? Or that you ignored our plans?"

He blew out a frustrated breath. "I wasn't thinking clearly." He ran a hand through his hair, clearly debating with himself in the silence that followed. "The phone call was from an ex I haven't seen or heard from since college."

She looked up at him in shock.

There was an ex who sent him reeling. That could only mean one thing. "She means something to you," Madison said, hearing her voice as if from a distance.

He inclined his head. "I thought she did once. It was a long time ago. I haven't spoken to her since college."

"This is the first time I'm hearing about her."

He swallowed hard. "We were together almost four years and I thought we'd be together through whatever happened with my career and hers." He didn't look at Madison as he spoke. "It turned out she was never comfortable with the idea of living my kind of life, the drafts and the potential trades to different cities. She wanted more, and she broke up with me after graduation."

Madison lowered herself into the nearest chair, unable to fully comprehend what he was telling her. The takeaway, however, was clear. He'd been in a serious relationship once. Had planned on spending his life with one woman. And he'd been so devastated when it ended he'd steered clear of serious relationships ever since.

"What does she want?" Madison asked.

"She left messages, all vague. She just said she wants to talk to me. She didn't say about what."

Madison nodded. "I see." And she did. A call from this woman was enough to have him pulling away from *her*.

"I don't think you do." He stalked over to her, bracing his hands on the arms of her chair.

He was too close, smelled too good, made her want too much.

"Hearing from Rachel brought me back to a bad place."

She swallowed hard. "I got that much."

"Not for the reasons you think. I'm not pining

over some lost love. Hearing from her reminds me that I wasn't good enough for her. Just like I wasn't good enough for Ian to want anything to do with me. Just like I'm no longer good enough to play ball." He swallowed, his strong throat working up and down. "I indulged in self-pity last night, and I hurt you in the process. I screwed up and I regret it."

Her hand rose of its own volition. She cupped his clean-shaven jaw in her palm and studied his sincere expression. She'd heard his words, understood he'd just bared his soul, and her heart softened despite her fear. And she was afraid. Every time she rebuilt her walls, when he chipped away at them, he took them down even farther. The fall would be that much harder when and if it came. But this ego-driven man had apologized to her twice, and she couldn't deny that showed change.

"I'm human, Angel." He let out a self-deprecating laugh, his face inches from hers.

"Yeah. I get that. And so am I." Which meant she could be hurt. So easily if he did a sudden one-eighty on her again.

"Am I forgiven?" he asked, his lips so close his breath feathered over her mouth.

"Yeah," she murmured, powerless against *this* Alex.

"Thank you." He leaned in and pressed his mouth

to hers.

She sighed and soaked up the seductive slide of his lips, the touch of their noses, the moment all the more intimate for the sweetness inherent in the kiss.

When he leaned back, her heart was pounding hard in her chest. "We're good?" he asked.

She treated him to a warm smile. "We're good," she assured him.

"Can we agree that what happens in the office doesn't come home with us?"

She closed her eyes, remembering that they had more to discuss and potentially disagree over.

"Agreed," she said on a sigh. Although she wished they could have stayed in the moment. But given that they were at work, he was right to bring them back to the issue at hand.

"Good. Because there's no way in hell that I can be the poster boy for weakness."

She closed her eyes and prayed for the words and strength to convince him otherwise.

SEVEN

Alex declared the PR plan off-limits for discussion, and Madison, Ian, and Riley had no choice but to respect his mandate, though Madison still hoped to change his mind. In her heart, she believed he could do a world of good to help people, not just in their campaign to train football players after their playing days but also high-school- and college-age players who should follow his lead and avoid risking further injury.

Their business trip to New York seemed to arrive overnight, and Madison was looking forward to seeing Manhattan. Olivia and Dylan, both in charge of team travel, also had meetings in New York City with the head of the hotel chain where the players stayed, and they all flew together on the corporate jet. Madison wasn't used to such high style, and though she prided herself on not being overly impressed by the wealthy lifestyle, even she was blown away by this luxury.

In the back of the small plane, Dylan and Olivia

had their heads together, conferring over something—although at times they appeared to be arguing rather than working. Madison turned away, wanting to respect their privacy and mind her own business.

Alex seemed preoccupied, looking out the window, so Madison closed her eyes, hoping to take a nap. Alex had kept her up late in the night, his hands everywhere on and in her body, as if he couldn't get enough. Heaven knew she couldn't. No matter what was going on in their personal lives, sexually they were completely compatible. She'd never had a man who read her so well or knew her so intimately.

Ever since that night they'd spent apart, he'd gone out of his way to be the attentive lover he'd been prior to his lapse. Madison didn't expect perfection from herself, let alone the man in her life, and she was all too happy to forgive him and move on. But that didn't mean she wasn't very aware of the ex-girlfriend he'd wanted to make his wife looming in the background, ready to return and wreak havoc with whatever it was she wanted.

Clearly, when Alex didn't want to deal with something, his method was to ignore it completely. Madison didn't find that an effective way to handle life, but it wasn't her place to judge. She just didn't like being in limbo, waiting for some proverbial shoe to fall.

The sensation of a hand on her thigh had her stirring, and she came to herself, realizing she must have fallen asleep. Her head rested on Alex's shoulder.

She forced her heavy eyelids to open and sat up, blinking to clear her vision.

"Hey, sleepyhead."

She laughed. "Someone kept me awake last night."

"I didn't hear you complaining."

"And you won't." She grinned. Then, remembering his preoccupation before she'd fallen asleep, her mood sobered. "Is everything okay? You seemed distracted earlier."

He nodded. "I just have a lot on my mind."

"Care to share? I'm a pretty good listener."

He leaned back in his seat and groaned. "Where to start? My agent left a message. He wants to know when I'm going to start thinking about things that can make me *real money,* like endorsements. What he really means is things that will make him money too." He scowled.

"What kind of deals does he think are open to you?"

"After my injury, he told me he could get me underwear ads." He held up a hand.

"Okay, I get it's not a power drink or sports equipment but…"

"It's trading on my face or body, not my accomplishments. It's just not something I want to do."

"Fair enough. I can't say I want to share that body with all of America either." Madison treated him to a sultry smile, reaching out to stroke his cheek.

Alex stilled, well aware this was the first time she'd acted possessive in any real way. The first time she'd felt comfortable reaching out to him as if she really was the other half of a couple. And he liked it.

He grasped her wrist. "That's not something you need to worry about." His voice sounded rough to his ears. She did that to him, aroused his protective caveman-like instincts.

"Glad to hear it."

He turned her wrist toward him and snaked his tongue along the pulse point. Her eyes grew hazy, and her pupils dilated. "If I slipped my hand into your pants, would I find you wet for me?"

Her lips parted, but no sound came out. "I'll take that as a yes," he said, running his lips along her bare arm.

A tremor rippled through her, and a glance at her breasts told him her nipples had hardened into tight peaks. Too bad he couldn't do anything about it here.

He leaned in and kissed her lips. "Now sit back and behave before our travel companions notice you're overheated and panting for me," he said with a grin.

She shot him a frustrated look and pulled herself

together, shifting in her seat as she glared at him. "You don't play fair," she muttered.

"Never said I did."

"Speaking of our traveling companions, have you noticed that Olivia and Dylan have been huddled back there since after we took off?" Madison asked.

He was glad to notice her voice trembled. She hadn't shaken off his effect on her that easily.

He shrugged. "They always seem to have something going on between them that nobody knows about."

"Hmm."

"Listen, while we're in New York, I'm going to see my cousin Gabe and his twin, Decklan. Gabe owns exclusive clubs in town, and I thought we could make a night of it. The four of us, if those two are interested." He jerked his thumb toward the back of the plane.

"Introducing me to family? Careful or I might get the wrong idea," she said, her tone teasing. But then, as if she realized what she'd said, her face paled. "I did not mean that like it sounded," she said, turning away, clearly unable to face him.

He shook his head. The frustrating woman still didn't believe he was serious about her. Convincing her was high on his list. He wasn't withdrawing at her joke, and he figured he'd just let his actions speak for him.

He grasped her hand in his and laid it on his lap, keeping her close for the remainder of the flight.

*   *   *

As a group, they checked into the hotel that normally hosted the Thunder when they played in the tri-state area. Dylan and Olivia stopped to say hello to the manager. Madison and Alex waited for their room keys. The plan was for the four of them to meet up for a late dinner.

"I still don't see why you need your own room," Alex muttered to her as he accepted the key card.

"Because this is a business trip, paid for by my employer, and I refuse to give them a hint of impropriety."

"That *them* you refer to is my half brother, who was sleeping with an employee before he married her," Alex reminded her.

"It's not the same thing." She wanted people at work to respect her. She wanted to respect herself. Sharing a room with Alex wouldn't accomplish that. "And it's not up for negotiation."

"Doesn't mean I won't be in your bed tonight," he said, pressing a kiss to the side of her neck before slipping his hand in hers.

She shivered at the seductive sensation of his lips

against her sensitive skin.

"Come. The elevators are over there," he said, not waiting for an answer, which was a good thing since she couldn't form a coherent word.

As they approached the wide bank of elevators, she heard someone call Alex by name. They both turned.

"Alex Dare?" A boy in a wheelchair came toward them, his father rushing to keep up with his excited son.

"Hi there," Alex said, striding up to the teenager.

"I'm a huge fan," he said, gushing.

"We're from Tampa," the father said.

"Yeah. We're in New York to see some doctors," the teen said in obvious distaste.

The older man looked down on his son wistfully but didn't say a word.

"Can I get an autograph?" the boy asked.

Alex grinned. "You sure can."

"Hang on. I'll go get paper from the front desk," Madison said, rushing over to the bell clerk and returning with a pen and paper.

"What's your name?" Alex asked, kneeling down to make himself level with the boy.

"Jake. Jake Wilton."

"Tell you what, Jake. I'll sign this, but I'll take your address and send you an autographed picture and some team memorabilia."

"All right!" The boy's cheeks flushed, and he grinned.

For the next few minutes, they exchanged information, and Alex signed the paper, to his *buddy*, Jake. Madison had never seen this side of Alex. True, she'd seen him with fans, but this exchange with the teenager was different. He was warm, caring, and so much more real.

She wondered if he ever wanted kids. It wasn't something she'd given much thought to, if only because she'd never found a man she wanted to settle down with. Those trust issues always reared their ugly head. But Alex, who had such an instant rapport with this boy, brought untapped feelings up inside her.

She glanced down. The two had their brown-haired heads close together as they had a private conversation she couldn't overhear.

"He's great with kids," the older man said, drawing Madison's attention.

"Yes, he really is." She smiled, her heart fluttering madly in her chest, and she wasn't sure why. She only knew something about this exchange touched her deeply.

Alex rose to his full height. "You'll remember what I said?" he asked the teen.

"Yes sir!"

Alex laughed. "Umm, no need to be formal."

Jake shot his father an *I told you so* look. "I knew you'd be cool," he said to Alex, looking up at him like he was his ultimate hero.

To Madison's surprise, Alex's cheeks turned red.

"It was great to meet you, Jake." Alex shook his hand as if he were an adult, leaving the teen beaming. He stepped over to the boy's father. "You've got a strong, brave son."

The other man's eyes grew watery. "Thank you. This ... today means a lot. He'll never forget this, and neither will I."

Alex shook his head, unsure what he'd done beyond the usual fan greeting, but he smiled anyway. "I won't forget him either," he told the older man.

And he meant it. The boy had struck a deep chord within him, and his young face and situation would stay with him for a long while. He walked toward the elevator, Madison beside him, lost in thought.

"Are you okay?" she asked.

He met her gaze. "I guess. It's just ... there but for the grace of God and all that." A car accident had put the boy in the chair, but life had its random moments that changed everything unexpectedly.

"How so?" Madison asked.

"If I'd been hit or fallen a different way, I could be in a chair too. All this time I've been wallowing in self-pity, as if not playing football was the worst thing that could have happened to me, when Jake will never have that chance at all. Never have chances at a lot of things I take for granted."

Madison slipped her smaller hand into his but didn't say anything, knowing when to keep silent. He squeezed her hand in gratitude, and they walked into the elevator.

* * *

Madison settled onto the edge of the king-sized bed in the large suite. A totally unnecessary expense, but everyone else seemed used to it, so she'd kept silent at check-in.

She waited for her luggage to be brought up so she could unpack her things, and she hoped they wouldn't be too badly wrinkled. Especially the dress she'd thrown in at the last minute just in case they went out for fun in Manhattan. Good thing, since apparently they were visiting Alex's cousin's nightclub.

When a knock came, she opened the door, expecting the bellman. Instead, Alex stood in the doorway, one arm braced on the molding.

"You're not the bellman." She stepped aside to let him in.

"Disappointed?" he asked, looking as off-kilter as he had when they'd stepped into the elevator earlier.

"Don't be silly. What's going on?"

He strode to the bed and flopped to his back, leaning against the pillows. "I just can't get Jake out of my head. He's so young, and he has to spend the rest of his life in a wheelchair, but he laughs and smiles like all's well with the world."

She sat on the bed and crawled over, cuddling against his hard body. He wrapped an arm around her and pulled her into him.

"You gave him something special to remember today. He met his hero, and you treated him like a normal kid. You were great with him," she murmured.

"Kids are so resilient and accepting. So much more so than adults," he said.

"That they are." She paused then said, "Focus on Jake's smile." She was at a loss how else to help him out of his funk.

"How did you get so smart?" He toyed with her hair, combing through the strands and twirling it with his finger.

She let out a sigh. "A lot of practice trying not to focus on bad things, I guess," she said, surprised she was answering so honestly.

"I want to know more about those bad things. More about you. The things you don't talk about," he said in a low, soothing voice.

She knew what he wanted. It was a story she rarely

told. Someone had to earn her trust and her heart before she'd even consider admitting that neither of her parents had wanted her. Saying it out loud made her vulnerable, and Madison normally didn't allow many people that close. She'd kept Alex at a distance the first time they were together, even as she'd known how hard she was falling in such a short time. Because she knew he wasn't a forever kind of guy, and the truth went to the deepest hurt she nursed in her heart.

But she could no longer hold back from this man. She didn't want to. He'd been asking for her trust, and if she was going to try, as he seemed to be doing, she had to let him in.

She sighed and said, "My mom left me and my dad. She said she was going to work one morning, and she never came back. When he realized something was wrong, he called her job, her friends, but no one had heard from her." She shrugged. "We didn't have any other family that I knew of, so it was just me and him."

He began to stroke her hair, long, soothing touches this time, keeping them connected as she spoke.

"How old were you?"

"I was twelve, and it was horrible. My father worked really long hours in construction and came home really late. Looking back, I know he went out drinking before coming home. I would let myself into the house after school, make myself dinner with whatever I could find in the fridge or the pantry, do my homework and … cry myself to sleep."

"Fuck," Alex muttered.

She was glad he couldn't see her face and appreciated the strength of his arms wrapped tightly around her. "One day he said we were going clothes shopping. I was really excited because, one, we never ever bought new things, and two, my clothes were getting tighter. I'd started developing and … you know."

She pulled in a deep breath, the lump in her throat so big it actually hurt. "You'd think this would get easier." She buried her face against his side.

"Take your time, Angel." His voice was warm and soothing, but she felt the tension emanating from him.

It wasn't an easy story to tell. It couldn't be an easy one to hear. Riley had cried when Madison had told her, and Madison had only given the other woman the bare bones.

My father dumped me at the mall, never to be seen again. The cold, clinical version. And even then, Madison hadn't wanted to face her friend after the revelation, but Riley had already inserted herself in Madison's life and wasn't going anywhere. She, more than anyone, had taught Madison what a true friend really was.

She lifted her head and drew a deep breath. "So we went to the mall. My father bought me a soda, and we wandered around the stores for a little while, and then he asked me if I needed to use the bathroom." Her body shook despite Alex's secure hold, the day coming back to her in vivid detail. "I went to the ladies' room, came out…" She couldn't say the words. To her mortification, a sob came out instead.

"That bastard," Alex said, his voice tight, anger evident beneath the surface.

He embraced her with his entire being, holding her close, but fury vibrated in his big, muscled body. Anger for her. She knew it without him having to explain, and the thought that he cared for her enough to feel that kind of emotion undid her completely. The protective walls that had always kept her apart and distant crumbled around her, and she *felt* things. Things she never wanted to experience again.

"No more," he said into her hair. "Don't relive it for me."

She normally didn't relive it at all. Didn't allow herself to remember the intense and all-encompassing pain and loss of that day and every one that followed. But now the dam had broken, and the memories flooded back, along with big, heaving sobs.

She'd walked out of the mall bathroom, looked around, and her dad had been nowhere to be found. She hadn't panicked. Not at first. She'd checked all the stores they'd been in. The men's stores. The food court. Finally she'd returned to the bathroom thinking maybe he'd gone back to find her. Some good Samaritan must have noticed the little girl sitting on the floor outside the restroom crying and called mall security. The rest was a blur, along with the ensuing years of her life spent in foster homes.

Alex didn't know how long she sobbed. From the way she cried, he figured it had been forever since she'd let her emotions free, and she exhausted herself in the process. The heavy sobs quieted first. Long after she grew silent, Alex held Madison in his arms, his heart beating hard in his chest. He'd wanted her to trust him, not unleash this kind of grief. Nausea filled him, along with pain that reached to the depths of his soul.

He stroked her hair, aware of the smallest hiccup or sound she made. Soon her breathing evened out, and he hoped to God she'd fallen asleep. A dreamless, memory-free sleep. She deserved as much.

But he couldn't stop his mind from spinning with the story she'd told, the things she'd said, and those she'd left out. Knowing about her past and hearing it from her lips were two very different things. More than anything, he wanted to hunt both her parents down and kill them with his bare hands. But he understood his rage wouldn't do Madison any good, and he'd have to get himself under control before she awoke.

When a knock sounded at the door, he slipped out from beside her and accepted her luggage, tipping the man quietly. Then Alex climbed back into bed and eased his arm around her once more.

In the peaceful silence, he couldn't help but look at his own life with more appreciation than he ever had before. His family was dysfunctional, but they were his. They were there. Day in and day out, he'd had people who loved him and who he could rely on. He had food to eat, a roof over his head, and though his father was a bastard of the first order, he'd always made sure he and his siblings never wanted for anything. Even Ian and his brothers and sisters hadn't been neglected.

Every child had a right to security and love, but the woman in his arms had had none of those things. She wouldn't want his pity, and in truth, he couldn't give it to her. Not when he admired her so damned much. She'd overcome her past and become a strong, independent woman. One he wanted to take care of and give everything she'd missed out on for all these years, especially the family she'd been denied.

Today had been an eye-opener on many levels, from the courageous teenager he'd met to the brave female he loved—

His thoughts screeched to a halt at the word that

had just run through his brain. Yet he couldn't deny it. For six months, he hadn't looked at another woman. In the last few weeks, he'd done all he could to show her he'd changed. Now he wanted to give her the security she'd never had and possess her completely. If that wasn't love, he didn't know what was.

* * *

Madison felt awkward after her emotional breakdown, but to Alex's credit, he didn't treat her any differently. She woke up to find the bellman had delivered her suitcase. Other than asking if she was okay, Alex had merely kissed her senseless and left her to get ready for dinner and clubbing afterwards. For her part, she was determined to put the episode behind her and move forward like she always did.

After dinner, they headed over to Elite, Alex's cousin's club. Olivia and Dylan headed for the bar while Alex looked for his cousin. They paused by the dance floor.

The club was elegant, glamorous, luxurious, and any other name Madison could think of for a New York City hot spot. Black ceiling, gold inlay etchings in the walls, leather banquettes, and open-air decks overlooking the main dance floor.

"According to the write-ups, when this place first opened, it cost three million." Alex shook his head.

"Thousand-dollar cover charges if the papers can be believed. Gabe doesn't talk."

Madison blinked in shock. "Just ... wow. But it is gorgeous."

"My cousin has good taste. So does his sister Lucy. She helped design the place."

Madison grinned and met his gaze. His dark eyes devoured her, and she did the same right back. He looked incredibly handsome in black pants and a white shirt, rolled at the sleeves. The unbuttoned shirt revealed tanned skin and gave her an enticing peek at his sprinkling of chest hair.

He looked over her shoulder, and a wide smile took hold. "There's Gabe." Alex led her to the private, roped-off area, his hand hot and branding on the small of her back, open thanks to a deep plunge in the material of her dress.

The private area was raised higher than the dance floor and bar, and Alex whistled over the music.

To her surprise, Gabe heard. He rose, disentangling himself from women who hung all over him, though she had to admit he looked bored with them all.

"Cousin!" Alex said as Gabe strode down a few steps and joined them. "Look at you up high so you can survey your kingdom."

Gabe's lips twitched but didn't lift in a full-blown

grin. In this, Madison could see distinct differences between Alex and Gabe. Gabe was more like Ian, more serious and always in control.

"It's about time you showed your face in New York." Gabe slapped Alex on the back. "Good to see you."

"Same. And thanks for coming to all those games. It was always good to have family there." Once learning about his other cousins, Gabe and his siblings welcomed them with open arms.

"My pleasure." He shifted his steely gaze to Madison. "Who is this?"

Approval laced his tone.

"Madison Evans." Alex snaked an arm around her waist in an unnecessarily proprietary gesture she actually liked. "Madison, this is my cousin Gabe."

She smiled at the man. "Nice to meet you, Gabe. Actually, I see a little family resemblance." She extended her hand, and Alex eased it down before tucking her even closer to his side.

Gabe chuckled. "So that's how it is."

"How what is?" Madison asked.

"I've seen you with women. This one's off-limits."

Before he could reply, Olivia walked over and threw her arms around him. "Hi there, cousin."

Madison realized that since Olivia and Alex shared a father, Gabe was the cousin of both of them.

"Hi, beautiful." Gabe hugged her tightly, light in his eyes as he looked her over. "Long time no see."

"Too long. It's a good thing business brought us to New York. Nice place you've got here." She gestured her hand wide, taking in the expanse of the club.

Pride glinted in his eyes. "I like it. You're all comped for the night, so enjoy. I'll come over to check on you later." With a nod of his head, he turned and walked away.

Madison blinked. "He's ... interesting. Very Ian-like."

Olivia, Ian's sibling, burst out laughing. "Well said! I knew I liked you." She hooked her arm into Madison's free one and pulled her away from Alex.

"Where are you taking her?" he asked, a scowl on his handsome face.

"For drinks and girl time. We'll see you gentlemen in a little while."

EIGHT

Madison found herself sitting at a small private table with Olivia, shots of tequila in front of her. Olivia worked as assistant travel secretary to the team. She also sat in on high-level meetings with Ian because he valued her advice and was training her in all aspects of team business. Madison didn't know her well, but Riley spoke highly of her, which vetted her enough for Madison. If she was going to drink with her and ultimately let down her guard, she needed that kind of assurance.

"To what do I owe the pleasure?" Madison asked, gesturing between them.

"I wanted to get to know you better," Olivia said.

"And take a breather from Dylan?"

Olivia laughed. "And now I know why Riley likes you." She raised her tequila glass. "Lick, salt, drink, and bite. Ready?"

"Oh good Lord, you're really going for this." Madison shrugged. One or two wouldn't kill her.

Madison licked her hand, salted, drank the burning liquid, and immediately bit into the lime wedge to kill the taste.

"Men are such a pain in the ass," Olivia said after pulling the lime from between her lips.

Madison's eyes watered, and she drew a deep breath. "They can be, yes. They can also be…" She turned her head and found Alex, leaning against a gleaming silver railing, his gaze never leaving her. "Hot." She turned back.

Olivia wrinkled her nose. "Exasperating. That's the word you were supposed to use. But it looks like my half brother got under your skin."

"The way Dylan's gotten under yours?" Madison asked.

Olivia gestured to another shot, and Madison drank along with her. "Damn men who want too much."

Madison shook her head and laughed, but the sound hurt. "That hasn't been my experience."

"I think it is now. Alex hasn't taken his eyes off of you since I pulled you away."

Her cheeks warmed, but Olivia was right. "Things are changing between us," Madison said, suddenly light-headed from the effects of the liquor.

"I've been close with Alex since I was a kid. When Avery gave Sienna her bone marrow, the kids got to know each other."

"Except Ian."

Olivia shrugged. "My big brother bore the weight for all of us. But Alex? It's been a long time since anyone but family saw him for just himself."

"I do," Madison whispered, thinking of the man who'd knelt down beside the teenager in the wheelchair. The man who'd held her as she'd bared her soul and relived her painful childhood. The man she wanted to feel filling her body tonight.

"I know. And I'm glad."

"What about you? Why are you leading Dylan around by his—"

Olivia waved her hand, cutting Madison off. "Is it that obvious?"

"No. It was just a guess based on what you've said. And not said. He seems like a decent guy."

"Let's dance," Olivia said, hauling Madison to her feet.

"There's a way to avoid answering," Madison muttered, thinking Olivia was more closed off than she was.

Before she could hit the dance floor, a pair of strong arms wrapped around her waist, lifted her into the air, and carried her to a darkened hallway before setting her down.

She turned, already knowing it was Alex. "What

was that for?"

He tilted her chin up and kissed her lips. "I'd had enough of your girl time."

She grinned and slid her arms around his neck. "Does that mean you missed me?"

"Always," he said, his voice a low rumble as he pulled her roughly against him. Her entire body vibrated with need.

"How long do we have to stay?" she asked, because it was his cousin's club, and she didn't want to be rude by suggesting they leave *now*. But she couldn't wait to be alone with him.

"We don't. Gabe's lending us his driver. We can get out of here any time."

"Now sounds good to me." She paused for them to say good-bye to Olivia and Dylan before Alex led her out the door.

A private limo and driver waited for them in front of Elite. And once inside the back of the limo, the privacy partition was raised. Alex leaned back in the seat, his arm stretched behind her. "I told him to drive around. I said I'd tell him when to head to the hotel," he said, his gaze leveled on hers.

"So we're free to do whatever we want back here?"

He nodded, his finger tracing the line of her dress down her cleavage and back up again on the other side. Her breasts grew heavy, nipples tightening, panties damp. Light music piped in around them, a beautiful melody she didn't recognize, but it added to the sexy atmosphere.

She knew what she wanted to do. Something she never initiated with any man because it indicated an intimacy she'd never felt before with anyone but Alex. And she felt it again now. More so than when they'd been together before even.

"I want my mouth on you," she murmured. Turning toward him, she reached for the button on his dark pants. He drew a sharp breath, eyes glittering with heat.

"You sure, Angel?" Alex asked, unable to tear his gaze from hers. The thought of her sucking him in her warm, wet mouth had his cock swelling and his body shaking with need.

"Completely." She slid off the seat and sank to her knees, then unzipped his pants.

He lifted his hips, and she hooked her fingers into his briefs and worked at his pants, until they fell to the floor around his feet. She maneuvered herself between his legs before capturing his hard cock in her hand.

He looked heavenward, praying for the strength not to come from her hot touch alone.

Eyes wide and focused, she slid her hand up and down his thick length, pausing to swipe a finger over the leaking pre-cum at the head. He let out a strangled groan. If she was going to experiment now, he would be in big trouble.

She bit down on her lower lip, studying him from various angles.

He wanted to bite that lip himself, then devour her mouth and thrust into her body—her mouth or her pussy, he didn't much care which, he thought, his hips arching up into her tight grasp.

"Not gonna pressure you, sweetheart but you have to do something, or this'll be over before you begin."

She leaned down and licked him experimentally. Heat shot through his groin, and he clenched his hands into tight fists. Anything to prevent himself from grabbing her by the hair and pumping into her mouth himself. She wanted to be in control, and he wanted to give her that.

Finally she parted her lips and took him in, enclosing him in moist heat. Fire licked at him from every angle as she ran her tongue up and down his shaft, lingering beneath the sensitive head before bringing him into her mouth so deep he hit the back of her throat.

She slid him out and in, her lips gliding then sucking him deep. With one hand gripping him and pumping up and down, she sucked him like a lollipop, cupping his balls in her free hand. He lost track of her moves and became a complete slave to sensation. His blood boiled in his veins, fucking stars flashed in front of his eyes, and he came so hard he lost track of everything but the unreal orgasm and the woman giving him such intense, all-consuming pleasure.

* * *

Madison woke early the next morning, her entire body aching in the best possible way from last night's *activities*. She stretched in delight. Looking over, she didn't see Alex. Instead, she saw a note on the pillow beside her.

She picked it up and read out loud. "Hey, beautiful. Went back to my room to shower. If I stayed, I'd have woken you up with my hands on your—" She blushed at the following words, fully aware he was right. If he'd joined her in the shower, they'd never get to breakfast and then their meeting on time. She'd definitely enjoy her morning more though.

She had to admit going with the flow was working for her. By spending time with Alex and not allowing herself to think about the future, she'd fallen into a routine she enjoyed. Much like last time except things were different now. *He* was different. He was attentive and focused on her. No distraction of media or attention to inflate his ego and pull him away from what was important and meaningful in his life.

She pulled out her phone and texted him, letting

him know that she was ready for breakfast. A few minutes later, she met up with him outside the elevator banks in the lobby.

He pulled her into his arms and kissed her like they'd been apart for days instead of a little over an hour. "Mmm. I could get used to this," she murmured against his mouth.

He stepped back and grinned. "You'd better because I don't plan on stopping anytime soon."

She linked her hand in his. "I need coffee desperately."

"And I need you." His looked into her eyes, gaze hot and heavy-lidded.

She swayed toward him, hoping he'd kiss her one more time.

"Excuse me. Alex?" A female voice interrupted them.

Madison turned to see a stunning brunette wearing a wine-colored skirt and matching jacket, waiting for him.

Alex stiffened. "What the hell? Are you following me?"

Madison narrowed her gaze, unsure who the woman was.

"I hate to interrupt—" the woman said.

"Then don't." Alex bit out his words in an ice-cold tone Madison had only heard once before, and everything inside her froze at the memory of him breaking up with her in his hospital room.

"Alex, please," the unknown female said.

"Go away."

The only woman Madison could imagine him speaking to that way now would be—

"*Rachel,* I believe me not returning your calls speaks for itself."

Madison closed her eyes, needing a minute to pull herself together to deal with this situation. She was facing the other woman who had meant something to him once. One he was still angry with and bitter over. Did that translate to him still having feelings for her? Nausea kicked in hard. She rubbed her hands against her own skirt, hoping she didn't look as nervous as she suddenly felt.

"I just need a few minutes of your time," Rachel said.

"I'm busy." He immediately pulled Madison closer to him. Today, his gesture of possession didn't feel as warm or intimate as it had last night. It felt necessary, like he needed to prove to this woman that he had moved on.

But had he? That was the question, and Madison suddenly felt chilled despite his body heat close beside her.

Madison swallowed hard. "Alex, go ahead. See

what she wants."

"Anything you have to say, you can say to us both. This is Madison—"

"Evans. I admire the work you're both doing with the Thunder."

Madison narrowed her gaze. How did Rachel know about her?

"How do you know what we're doing?" Alex asked before Madison had the chance.

"I have a proposal for you, and before I put it together, I had to know what I was up against." It was hard to know if she meant in business or his personal life, since she looked Madison over before settling her stare on Alex once more.

"How did you know where we were?" he asked.

"You weren't answering your cell—"

"A number you shouldn't have had either."

"I have sources. Anyway, I called the Thunder front office and asked how to get in touch with you. I'm based in New York. I have been since graduation. When they said you were here in the city, I managed to get the hotel name and decided I'd come to see you in person. I was on my way up to your room."

Neither of them asked how she'd gotten her hands on that. She'd already said she had *sources*.

"You can talk in front of Madison," Alex said. His frown didn't ease, and his entire body was stiff beside hers.

Madison shook her head. "No. You go hear what Rachel has to say. I'll meet you at our meeting." She stepped out of his embrace and away from his touch.

"Madison," he said on a low, unhappy growl.

She moved, putting a hand on his shoulder and whispering so only he could hear. "It's called closure, and something tells me you need it. Go hear her out."

Alex grumbled, arguing until he realized she wouldn't give in. "Fine," he muttered.

Madison walked away, her stomach in knots, her heart thudding painfully against her chest. But she had no doubt she'd done the right thing. Rachel's actions had defined Alex's entire adult life. He needed to come to terms with her rejection. Not to mention, he needed to hear her proposal now and process it alone, without Madison there to cloud his judgment or, heaven forbid, provide him with guilt should he still respond to the attractive woman from his past.

If Madison wanted a future with Alex, and God help her she did, she needed him free and clear of his past and his demons. And free of whatever grip Rachel still held after all these years.

* * *

Alex sat down in the hotel restaurant across from Rachel. He didn't want to be here. He had no desire to sit across from the woman who'd broken his heart and talk about anything. And if he had to be here, he preferred Madison be by his side. He didn't like the look on her face when she'd told him to go with Rachel.

He ordered coffee and an omelet and waited for her to do the talking. For his part, he had nothing to say. In the ensuing silence, he studied her, noting she'd aged well. Her brown hair was shorter but suited her features. But looking at her now, nothing stirred inside him. Not desire, lust, or even mild wanting. To his amazement, he didn't even feel regret for what might have been.

So why the hell are you so angry? a voice that sounded too much like Madison asked.

Pride, his own internal voice answered. Rachel had hurt his pride by breaking up with him because the life he'd offered wasn't good enough for her. He hadn't been good enough for her. Now? He didn't give a shit.

"Okay, let's hear it," he said, giving in and breaking the silence. "What's so important that you had to track me down here?"

"How have you been?" she asked.

Great. She wanted to make small talk. "I've been wonderful. Drafted, MVP, fantastic career until I got knocked in the head a few too many times. But I've got a new career path, and all's well." He folded his arms across his chest.

She pinned him with her knowing stare, still silent.

He bit the inside of his cheek. "How have you been?" he asked in return.

She smiled. "Fine, thanks. I moved to New York after we graduated. I got a job with an entertainment firm and worked my way up the ladder. I married a Wall Street guy. It was good until it wasn't. We were divorced last year. I made partner at my firm … and here I am." She spread her hands out in front of her.

Wall Street. "Well, you got the guy who wore a suit and tie and went into work every day in the same place, same state. Sorry it didn't work out," he said, surprised he meant it.

"It happens." She shrugged. "You know, Alex, I've always had one regret."

He found it difficult to swallow. "Yeah? What's that?"

"The way we ended. I wish I'd had the courage to tell you all along I didn't have it in me to be the wife of a ball player. But we got serious so quickly, and because your family lived in Florida, I met them, spent time with them. That put a more intense spin on things. And I didn't know how to get out of it by then."

She twisted the napkin between her hands, not meeting his gaze. "Honestly, while we were in school,

I didn't *want* out of it. But suddenly there was graduation, pro offers, and the draft, and you were *proposing*. I wasn't ready for it."

"It's not like you didn't know I was thinking about it," he said, reminding her he hadn't exactly kept his feelings to himself. And she hadn't argued with his ideas about how they could stay together.

But she hadn't offered any of her own either, he realized, looking back.

"No. You were always up front. It was me. And I'm sorry." She forced her eyes up to meet his. "I always regretted not being honest with you, with myself. I've carried that burden for years."

Despite the anger he'd harbored, he felt himself softening toward her. After all this time, did it really matter? They'd each gone their own way, lived their own life. She obviously wanted some sort of forgiveness.

And Madison wanted him to have closure. He had to admit his chest felt lighter, having heard Rachel's honest words. "It's in the past," he heard himself saying. "We should both let it go."

He'd always believed she wasn't a bad person. That anger was about his bruised ego more than anything else, and he'd only let it fester and grow over time, infecting how he'd treated women and his ideas about relationships.

"I needed to hear that," she said. "And I actually think you mean it."

"I never say things I don't mean." That much hadn't changed.

"Okay then. If we're back on friendly ground—"

"I didn't say we were friends."

She smiled anyway. "We're not adversaries then. That should make my proposal easier for you to hear. Without that anger between us."

He ran a hand over his face. "Let's hear it. I have a meeting in twenty minutes."

She smiled. "Like I said, I'm a partner at an entertainment company." She handed him her card. "And we're working with S&E Network. Sports and Entertainment Network," she elaborated. "They want to hire you for a sports show with Allison Edwards, the sports commentator. They'd like you to come in and test with her, but from the way they're talking, if you want the job, it's yours."

He blinked. A job offer was the last thing he'd expected from Rachel. Then again, he'd had no idea what she'd wanted.

"It's a great opportunity," she said. "For one thing, it's national. You'd be back in the spotlight, and we both know how much you liked to feed on that adrenaline and energy."

Even back in college, he'd enjoyed the attention

and social perks that came with being a star athlete. He couldn't accept anything from sponsors back then, but as his professional career had grown, he couldn't deny he'd lived large and loved every minute.

It helped keep the loneliness away and didn't give him time to think about the things in life he'd decided he would never have, like a serious woman and a family of his own. He'd been so angry at Rachel he'd turned his back on so much, he realized. Things he now wanted and not with the woman sitting here.

He shook his head, bringing himself back to the present. "Did you run this by my agent?" he asked.

She shook her head and grinned. "He said you were being an ass and I should try to get through to you."

"He did not." Although knowing Kevin Falcon and how pissed he was, maybe he had.

"Actually, he said he'd like to mention it to you but not to get my hopes up because you weren't entertaining offers these days—or returning his calls. After I said you and I went way back and maybe I could pitch it to you myself, then yeah. He did say exactly that."

Alex shook his head and laughed. "That bastard."

"Sounds like you've been giving him your share of grief."

He leaned back in his chair and nodded. "Could be."

"I'm sorry about that last hit. I know how much football means to you."

Alex stiffened. He didn't want to get into his feelings with her. "Thank you."

"So about the offer, I can send something in writing over to your agent if you're interested."

And wasn't that the question. Was he interested?

* * *

Madison feigned interest in the interview with the Wall Street financial advisor they were trying to bring on board to meet with the players on a regular basis. Helping the guys with their finances from the beginning of their careers would teach them fiscal responsibility and remind them to think of the future when spending or not spending their often substantial incomes.

She was able to give her speech to the man by rote, then she turned to Alex to bolster things with the personal touch, the story of a man whose career had been cut short and how good financial advice had kept him from being broke now. Because he hadn't already blown through all the money in his bank account, he'd had time to think about his post-injury options without making decisions while in panic mode. Something they wanted the financial advisor to impress upon the players. Then teach them how to save.

But her mind wasn't on business. It was on what had gone on between Alex and Rachel at breakfast. Her head pounded, and the small, windowless conference room they'd rented for the interview didn't help. She felt as if the walls and her life were closing in on her. Although she hadn't seen any sexual interest in Alex's eyes when he'd looked at his one-time girl-friend, his remaining anger told her there were still feelings there. The thought hurt, but it was true.

She'd had to give him the freedom to explore those emotions and work through them in whatever way he needed. She hadn't seen a ring on the other woman's hand, indicating she was, at the very least, not married. Which left all the other woman's options open too.

Madison's temple throbbed, and she was grateful when Bill Akins spoke, ending the meeting. "Well, it was a pleasure meeting you both. I need some time to think about your offer. The travel involved will impact my family, so I have to run this by my wife before making any decisions."

"We understand," Madison said, gathering her things and placing them in her larger purse.

"And we look forward to hearing from you," Alex told him. "Hopefully with a yes, you'd love to come on board."

The other man walked out and shut the door behind him.

"Well, that went well," Madison said. "Hopefully he'll agree." She hiked her purse over her shoulder. "I think I'm going to go back to the room and lie down. I have a headache."

"Can I get you something for it?" Alex asked, concern in his voice.

"No, thanks. I'll just go upstairs and rest." She started for the door.

"Aren't you going to ask what happened at breakfast?" His deep voice and that question stopped her.

As much as she wanted to know what had gone on with Rachel, a part of her dreaded the truth, fearing the other woman's return would have to change things between her and Alex on some level.

She swallowed hard. "Sure, I'll listen. If you want to tell me."

"Madison." Her name sounded on a low rumble.

"What?"

He held her gaze. "I didn't think we played that way."

Uncomfortable now, she fiddled with her bag strap and laid the heavy bag on the table. "I don't know what you're talking about."

He cocked an eyebrow. "Games. Distrust. I thought we were open and honest with each other."

She nodded. But her thoughts were slamming around in her head at a rapid pace. The one that stuck out was her biggest weakness. When she'd rekindled this relationship, the one thing she'd promised herself was that she'd be the one to walk away first. She'd meant it then. Now it would be that much harder, knowing how deeply she was already involved. But if she got even an inkling that Alex was still interested in his old girlfriend, she would gather her pride and walk away, head held high.

She straightened her shoulders and met his gaze. "Fine. What happened with Rachel? I want to know."

"Finally something honest." He strode to the door and turned the lock, taking her by surprise. He then settled into the big conference room chair and pulled her into his lap.

"Alex—" She squirmed in his lap, but he held on tight. His body was warm and hard, his arms around her solid and safe. She wanted everything with him so badly. And she wanted him for a lot longer than a brief sexual affair.

Somehow she'd given him her heart, and she feared he'd break it again. Whether he meant to or not. She swallowed a pain-filled moan.

He eyed her warily, but he kept his hold on her firm. "You were right saying I needed closure. I realized all that anger I held on to was more about my bruised ego than hurt feelings. It embarrassed me to have given everything so freely and have her throw it all back in my face."

She wasn't surprised he'd come to a revelation. She'd wanted that for him so he could let go of the past for good.

"And Rachel," he went on. "It turns out she's always regretted that she didn't have the guts when we were together to tell me how she really felt about my career and my future plans."

Madison managed a laugh. "Yeah, well, you're a pretty tough guy to go up against when you want to be."

"I do try." He grinned, a panty-moistening grin that had her shifting around in his lap. "I didn't make it easy for her apparently," he said, sobering. "She'd met my family by then, knew I was serious..." He shrugged it all off. "Anyway, I guess realizing it was more a question of my bruised ego than me nursing a broken heart helped me finally put it behind me."

Unable not to, she looped her arms around his neck. "I'm glad. Is that what Rachel wanted too? To make peace with the past?"

He drew a deep breath, making all Madison's nerves go haywire. "No. There's more," he said, confirming her fear.

Madison stiffened. "She wants you back?" She

blurted out the first thing that came to mind.

"No! Not that way!"

She let out a long, relieved breath. Of course, if she didn't want him back, there was something wrong with the woman, Madison thought, unsure if she should believe Rachel didn't have a hidden personal agenda.

Reminding herself Rachel had given him up willingly once before, she forced herself to focus. "Then what does she want from you?"

"She works at an entertainment company that is partnering with Sports and Entertainment Network. They want me to test with Allison Edwards for a sports show. National TV," he said, clearly still surprised by the offer.

But according to the gleam in his eye, he wasn't adverse to the idea. In fact, Madison guessed there was something inherently appealing about the exposure of a national television show to a competitive, driven man like Alex.

"What did you tell her?"

"She said I should take some time and think about it. I didn't have to say much of anything."

"Are you going to consider taking the job?" Madison asked.

The long silence that followed was answer enough.

He tilted her chin up, his gaze soft on hers. The intensity in his dark eyes made it clear he didn't find this any easier than she did. Which didn't seem to help her frayed emotions, and brought her close to the edge of tears.

He slid one hand to the back of her head, pulling her in close and kissing her. Not in the command-and-take-charge way that he usually did. He took his time, gliding his lips over hers and tracing them lightly with his tongue, back and forth, teasingly, before sliding inside. Whatever point he'd been trying to make was lost in the emotion of what should have been a simple kiss.

It wasn't.

The banked fire always present exploded between them, and suddenly his mouth on hers wasn't enough. With a moan, she shifted in his lap, reveling in the pressure of his swollen cock against her pulsing, needy sex.

"Shit, Angel. You feel so fucking good. So hot," he said, raising his hips in time to her movements.

The hard bulge of his erection came into direct contact with her clit, and waves of pleasure swept through her body, but more frightening were the feelings of pure need and love that accompanied the physical rush. No, she thought, as if wishing the love away would change the emotion.

"I bet if I slipped my hand into those panties, you'd be wet for me, wouldn't you?"

She moaned at the image he created. Yes, she'd be wet. She was soaked now.

As if to test his theory, he slid a hand beneath her skirt, his fingers easing beneath her panties and parting her slick folds.

"Yes," he groaned as her hips arched, pressing her sex into his touch.

The glide and press of his roughened fingertip had her trembling inside and out.

"I need to be inside you."

"Here?" she squeaked.

"Locked door, no windows. Fuck yes." He stood, easing her onto her feet. With one hand, he swept her purse and the remaining papers he'd had out onto the floor.

Unwilling to think any further, let alone argue, she rose and unbuttoned her skirt. Let it fall. His gaze darkened at the sight that greeted him, and his hot stare made her even wetter.

"Let me help," he muttered, fingering the bow at her hips. "This is my favorite pair of yours." He lifted her onto the table. She raised herself up so he could remove her underwear, and she watched in shock as he stuffed them into his pocket.

He merely grinned and rid himself of his jacket, then dropped his pants, boxer briefs along with them. She stared at his penis, so long, thick, and ready to glide into her, and her sex clenched at the thought.

He stepped between her legs, his large hands holding her thighs apart, and stared down at her. "I love how you look, so wet for me. So ready." He nudged her opening with the head of his cock.

She moaned out loud.

"That's it. Let me hear you, baby."

She bit down on the inside of her cheek. "But someone else might too."

"Let 'em be jealous then." A devilish grin lifted his lips.

She rolled her eyes at his arrogance. Then he gripped the flesh on her thighs harder, and her eyes rolled for a different reason as he parted her folds and thrust in deep.

"Alex," she moaned at the invasion that was hard and thick, pulsing inside her.

He pulled out only to plunge back in, the force of his movement sliding her backwards on the cool polished wood of the table.

"Can't wait. I've got to come."

His words caused a rippling of desire to shoot from her depths where they joined to other, unrelated parts. Never before had sex encompassed every inch of her body, but it did now.

Every thrust, grind, glide out, and hard push back into her caused sparks of electricity to reach outward, and she felt Alex from the tips of her toes to the lump in her throat and beyond to the stars that burst brightly behind her eyes.

He picked up a steady rhythm, each drive into her accompanied by the arousing roll of his pubic bone against her sex. She glanced at his handsome face, jaw tight, eyes narrowed and focused. On her. Without warning, he slowed down and raised her into a half-sitting position on the table. She rested on her elbows as he rolled his hips, keeping their bodies in direct contact that was so hot and intimate. He deliberately ground directly on her clit, causing those stars behind her eyes to burst as he rocked them both to the most earth-shattering orgasm she'd ever experienced.

Tremors and vibrations shook her long after he'd spent himself inside her. No condom again, and she couldn't bring herself to care. Everything about this moment was surreal, something more out of a novel than real life, and she knew she'd take this memory out and relive it time and time again.

Later, when she thought about the job offer he'd received, reality broke through the sensual bubble he'd put her in. Because Rachel had offered him fame again. He'd been used to the attention and accompanying perks before having it suddenly ripped away. And it had been the lack of those things that had led him back to Madison. To proclamations of wanting a relationship, to the changes she'd seen in his entire personality since his forced retirement.

What would happen if he returned to that life? To the hoards of fans, the women ... Would she lose him all over again? Madison's stomach did a complete one-hundred-eighty-degree flip at the thought, and everything inside her grew cold. The truth was, everybody ultimately left her, and she'd be better off preparing for the eventuality with Alex sooner rather than later.

NINE

Madison returned to Miami and a normal routine. She worked, spent nights with Alex, and dealt with prep for the upcoming hearing about her foster mother. Jonathan was thorough in questioning her and keeping her in the loop about what to expect. His private investigator hadn't found anything on Eric to help their case, indicating her foster brother had been very careful. No way did Madison believe he was clean or operating in his mother's best interest. The hearing was in two weeks, and she scheduled a final meeting the week before with Jonathon, who wanted to run Q and A by her one last time.

She tried hard not to think about what could possibly come up at the hearing, pushing it away into a box in the back of her mind until she needed to open it and deal with the contents. It was the way one of her social workers had taught her to deal with long-term problems when she was a child, and the method had

191

stuck.

In the meantime, life went on. To her surprise, Alex had invited her to his mother's house for dinner this coming weekend, and despite her nerves, she'd agreed.

There was no further discussion about Rachel or the job offer, and the wondering niggled at the back of Madison's mind. She still wanted him to consider the PR campaign proposed by Derek Fine, but she knew better than to think he'd be receptive now. Especially when he had another offer on the table.

She stared at the inside of her closet, attempting to pick a dress to meet her boyfriend's mother. Wasn't that a first? she mused. In all her relationships, none had progressed to the point where she'd met the parents. She had met Alex's other side of the family when they'd dated, more because of Riley than Alex's instigation. She hadn't met his full siblings or parents, and she shivered, glad Riley and Ian would be there offering familiarity and support.

Even she knew what a big deal it was for Alex to bring a woman home, especially after he'd mentioned he'd done the same with Rachel. She pushed thoughts of the other woman away. Again. Madison's insecurities were just that, her own. Alex had given her no reason to let them interfere in the present. She'd counseled enough women over the years to know how to talk to herself and keep herself looking forward, not back. She found the more she kept thinking positively, the easier it became to continue on that way.

She chose a pastel-printed sundress along with a tasseled pair of sandals. Because of the heat and humidity, she pinned her hair up in a loose bun, letting soft strands fall to her shoulders. A spritz of light perfume, a swipe of blush, some lip gloss and she was as ready as she'd ever be. It certainly was the most she'd angsted over clothing choice, she thought wryly.

Her doorbell rang just as she'd changed her purse to something small she could slip over her shoulder. Drawing a deep breath, she headed to answer the door for Alex, who'd showered and changed at home after a trip to the gym.

She answered the door, her gaze drifting over his fine form, a pair of khaki cargo shorts, and docksiders on his feet, a light blue collared short-sleeve polo shirt accenting his tanned skin and brown eyes.

His gaze skimmed over her in return, those chocolate eyes darkening. "You look beautiful, Angel."

She felt herself blushing. "Thank you. You look pretty hot yourself."

He grinned. "Ready?"

She nodded. "Just let me grab my purse and the gift."

He shook his head. "You didn't have to buy them

anything."

"I can't show up at your parents' house empty-handed! What will they think of me?" She stepped into the entry, where she'd left her bag, keys, and a small arrangement of flowers.

"They'll think you're amazing just like I do." He came up behind her, wrapping his arms around her waist. "Damn, baby, you're nervous?"

She turned to face him, their bodies in intimate contact, her gaze close to his. "Your father owns one of the most luxurious hotels in Miami. Your mother's been photographed in magazines with him. She's gorgeous. And you're their oldest son. Yes, I'm nervous!"

He smoothed his thumb over her lower lip, replacing her nerves with desire. "They're going to love you just like I do," he assured her, his gaze hot on hers.

She swallowed hard, not knowing how deeply to read into those words. They weren't *I love you* per se, and yet her heart kicked up a silly rhythm of excitement and hope. Damn, how she hated hope. It always knocked her on her ass. And yet … it remained.

A forty-minute drive later, thanks to traffic, they arrived at a well-kept home in a regular neighborhood, similar to Franny and Daniel Grayson's. Ian's car was already in the driveway, and Alex pulled up behind him. She stared at the house in silence, trying to process the difference in what she saw and what she'd expected.

"You okay?" Alex asked.

"Yes. I'm just surprised. I thought the place would be bigger."

"Grander?" he asked, a grin on his face.

"Well … yes."

He let out an amused chuckle. "Galls my father to no end. His home with Ian's mother was like a mansion. It turns out, at first, he put Mom up in a regular house so nobody would suspect she was an important man's mistress." He snorted, letting her know what he thought of that situation. "Later, when they married, my mother refused to change her lifestyle or ours. She didn't want us spoiled by money."

Madison shook her head and smiled. "Turns out your chosen career did that instead."

He tipped his head back and laughed. "Never thought of it that way, but you're right. Then it took it all away just as quickly, which is why I appreciate my mother's down-to-earth ways."

"Yet you kept the Porsche," she said, patting the dashboard lightly.

"A man's gotta have his toys and some luxuries."

She caught his wink and grinned, unable to resist him when he was playful and fun. Okay, she was never able to resist him.

"Ready to go in?"

She blew out a long breath and smiled. "Actually, I am."

He led her up the front path, surrounded by perfectly manicured greenery and flowers. He knocked once and pushed open the door.

Alex's mother greeted them as soon as they stepped inside. Madison recognized the beautiful woman from the photo shoot in a local magazine that had spotlighted her devotion to charitable causes.

"Alex!" She wrapped her arms around her son, pulling him in for a motherly hug.

"Hi, Mom." He hugged her back before easing out of her embrace.

"It's been too long," she chided him. "It's about time you stopped hiding from the world. And is this the woman I have to thank?"

Madison blushed, certain she hadn't had anything to do with that change in Alex. More likely, it was Ian's job that had given him purpose again and made him feel worthwhile.

"Mom, this is—"

"Madison! I know. I've heard all about you from Riley and of course from the little I could pry out of my son." She stepped over to Madison and grasped her free hand. "It's so wonderful to meet you."

"I feel the same way, Mrs. Dare."

"Oh my goodness, call me Savannah, please." She squeezed Madison's hand and released her.

Madison blinked. Alex had been right. She liked his mother already for making her feel comfortable immediately. She'd expected a staid, Palm Beach type of socialite. Instead of a set, trendy bob, her blonde highlighted hair fell past her shoulders, and although she wore a sundress, on her feet were flats, not heels. There was no air of pretense to be found.

Instead, Savannah Dare was real. Madison breathed out a sigh of relief and held out the flowers. "Thank you for inviting me today."

Savannah smiled, giving Madison a glimpse of an expression similar to her son's. "These are beautiful." She paused to sniff the fragrant blooms. "Thank you, although you really shouldn't have. Now come inside, you two. The rest of the family is in the great room. Unfortunately, your father had an emergency at the hotel, so he'll be back in a little while."

Alex led Madison inside, his hand on her back, a position she was beginning to anticipate and get used to. She relaxed when he laid his hand on the base of her spine, and she'd long since stopped cautioning herself not to, even if the occasional thought did pop out as a warning. She was getting better at trying to accept things when they were good. Not so much at stopping the notion of anticipating the other shoe falling.

Alex introduced her to Sienna, his baby sister, now almost twenty-one years old.

The young woman was a bouncing ball of energy, blonde like her mother, with Alex's dark brown eyes. She immediately began a not-so-subtle get-to-know-you session that consisted of her peppering Madison with questions.

"So how old are you?" Sienna asked.

Alex shot his sister a glare.

"My God, your mother would smack you for being rude," Riley said, joining them. She grinned at Madison.

"What? I'm almost twenty-one," Sienna said, as if that would help.

Madison bit the inside of her cheek so as not to laugh. "It's okay. I'm twenty-six."

"And where did you go to school?"

"I did my undergrad at Lynn University, and I got my MSW at the University of South Florida."

"What's an MSW?" Sienna asked.

"Master of Social Work."

"I'm graduating with a bachelor's in management, but I have no idea what I want to do with my life. I just know I want to experience everything," she said with the exuberance of the truly young and carefree, and who'd nearly lost it all.

"I hope you do. And you certainly have time and options," Madison assured the girl.

"Oh! Dad's here," Sienna said, waving at the tall man who entered the room before she turned back to Madison without missing a beat. "What about your family, Madison? Are you from Florida? Do your parents live here?"

Madison opened and closed her mouth, but no words came out.

Riley's mouth opened in a silent O.

"Dammit, Sienna." Alex grasped Madison's hand.

She pulled herself free. She'd been around enough to know this question came up in different situations. "I was born in Miami, but my parents no longer live here." She smiled to alleviate everyone else's tension.

"Oh. Where—"

"Done," Alex said, gripping Madison's hand and pulling her away. "Sorry," he said when they were alone.

"There's no reason to be. Those are perfectly normal questions. I have my standard answers. It's fine."

He met her gaze, admiration that made her uncomfortable staring back at her.

"Alex, have you offered Madison some of my tea? It's really the best, if I do say so myself," his mother said, breaking into their conversation.

Madison smiled in relief. "I'd love some tea."

"I made it just this morning. None of that premade stuff my son keeps on hand." She wrinkled her nose. "Alex, go introduce Madison to your father. I'll be right back with some glasses for everyone."

"Come on," Alex said. He led her next to his father, who stood with his brother, Jason. Introductions were quick. "It's a pleasure to meet you both," Madison said, noting the similarities in all the Dare men. Tall, dark, and handsome wasn't a cliché when it came to them.

"I've been looking forward to meeting the girl who has tamed my brother." Jason lifted his glass to Madison.

Alex rolled his eyes.

"The right woman will do that to you, son. Just you wait," Robert said to Jason.

Then he turned his gaze on Madison. He possessed the same steely-gray gaze as Ian, although his was a touch warmer. "It's a pleasure to meet you. Alex tells me you're working together with the Thunder?"

She nodded. "He's been a real asset with the players and the program we're instituting."

Robert smiled. "Wonderful. He needed a distraction from things. And what's this I hear about a television offer?"

Madison's stomach cramped at the enthusiasm in

the older man's tone.

"It's just an offer," Alex said. "No decisions have been made."

"I'd think it would be a no-brainer. You love the spotlight. Hell, you were born for it," Robert said, slapping his son on the back. "Whether it's on the football field or in front of a camera, you love being in the thick of things."

"I was going to talk to Jace about it later." Alex caught sight of Ian making his way toward them. "And I'd rather not discuss it now." He wasn't ready to tell Ian he might leave the team before he'd really begun to make an impact.

He winced at the thought. Just one of the things keeping him up at night. Another was the woman suddenly stiff by his side. She didn't like the idea of him returning to the spotlight any more than his half brother would, albeit for different and, for now, unknown reasons. He'd yet to determine what was really bothering Madison about the possible job. She'd all but clammed up on him, so he'd dropped the subject. Until he made a decision one way or another, he didn't need to manufacture issues between them.

The rest of day went better than he could have hoped. And if he'd waited for a hint of anxiety to overtake him while Madison was accepted by his family, none came. Later, he walked into his place, where they'd agreed to sleep tonight. Though he couldn't believe he'd reached the point in his life where he had a woman's clothing hanging in his closet and his in hers, one look at Madison's expressive, beautiful face and he knew exactly why every damned thing about this was okay.

Which made the talk he needed to have with her now so damned hard. But talking to his brother had helped him focus and see what he wanted and needed in his life. She was a part of that. The biggest part.

Alex tossed his keys onto the shelf near the door and met up with Madison in the living room. "Have fun today?" he asked.

She smiled. "I had a great time. Your family's amazing. You're all so close."

"I know. We're lucky." He clasped her hand. "And you really made an impact. Mom wants you back soon. Jace would steal you if he could."

She laughed at his obvious exaggeration.

"Umm, can we talk?"

"Sure." She gestured toward the sofa, and he joined her, sitting down next to her. "What's up?"

"You know I had a long talk with Jace today, right?"

She nodded. "You two looked like it was an intense conversation. I'm assuming it was about the job offer. Honestly, I'm good with whatever you decide," she said.

"Really?" He hadn't expected it to be so easy, and he wasn't convinced she meant it.

She met his gaze and nodded. "Do it. Take the job. It's perfect for you. You can get back the status and fame you love." She didn't waver, but he could see how hard she fought back showing emotion.

He grasped her hands. "I want to test. That's all. Just to see how I like it. For all I know, it's not for me. Or maybe they'll hate my performance."

She laughed at that. "Not likely."

"You never know," he said with a shrug. "You're really okay with it?"

She managed a smile he sensed was forced. "I do. I get why you need to do this."

"You look like you're trying your best to be enthusiastic, but I know you. What's going on?"

She leaned back against the couch and sighed. "I think we're building something important for players. It'll be a loss there if you leave, but you can't stay with one thing when you'd rather be doing something else."

He narrowed his gaze. He believed their job was part of what was going on in that head of hers, but it wasn't everything. He also sensed she wouldn't be admitting anything to him now.

"Look, I still don't know the details about this gig. It could be football season only. It could be weekends only. Maybe I could do what Strahan does and commute and keep this job too." There were a ton of variables, none of which he knew. Although he'd put a call in to his agent to get them, right now everything hinged on the test.

He hoped that didn't include his relationship with Madison as well.

* * *

The ringing of her cell phone jarred Madison out of a deep sleep. She rolled over, knocking the phone off the nightstand before finally picking it up to answer. "Hello?"

"Ms. Evans?"

"Speaking."

"This is Darla from the Hudson Arms nursing home."

Completely awake now, Madison sat upright in bed. "Is something wrong?"

Alex stepped out of the shower, a towel wrapped around his waist. "Who's on the phone?"

She held up a hand.

"I'm sorry, can you repeat that?"

The woman at the nursing home spoke. "Her son, Eric, came by at an ungodly hour. Since Franny was awake, we let him come in. He upset her terribly. We weren't able to calm her down and had to call the doctor in to give her a light sedative."

Madison swallowed hard. "I'll be right over."

"Well, she's sleeping now. We just felt we should notify you."

"You did the right thing. Where is Eric now?"

"He left but promised he'd be back."

"I'll talk to my lawyer and see what I can do. Thanks for calling. And I will be by later." She disconnected the call and met Alex's gaze.

"Problem?" He ran a towel over his damp hair.

"I need to call Jon. I think I need a restraining order to keep Eric away from his mother. Can I get that on her behalf?"

"If the doctors are willing to testify he's a danger to her health, I'm sure you can. Maybe you can get the hearing moved up. Do you want to head over to the nursing home now?"

She nodded, still in shock over the phone call. "I suppose I should check on her. I can't call Jon till nine a.m. anyway."

"Well, we could, but you're right. Let's wait till he gets to the office. Go jump in the shower. I'll pour you some coffee, and we can get moving."

"You don't need to come with me."

"I want to. You met my family. I'd like to meet yours."

"Franny is not my family." She bit her cheek. "I'm

sorry. That came out wrong."

He narrowed his gaze, but she went on before he could react to that telling statement.

"But the truth is, she probably won't even know *me*, so what's the point of trying to introduce you?"

"What's the point of denying you care about her? Or that she's the only family you have left and it hurts you to lose her?" He sat down beside her, his body warm from the shower, his scent clean and strong.

She met his gaze. "You don't get it," she said, frustrated. She attempted to rise to her feet, but he grasped her hand.

"You're wrong. I do." He pulled her back down beside him. "You've had way too much loss and pain in your life. And I contributed to that," he said, his voice rough with regret. "But if you don't start to ease up and trust in the people around you now, you're going to end up—"

"Say it," she said, folding her arms across her chest to ward off the sudden chill.

He shook his head and rose, walking back into the bathroom and closing the door. He didn't have to use the words for her to know what he meant.

She was going to end up alone.

*   *   *

The nursing home was clean and the staff pleasant and

accommodating, Alex thought, but he was still depressed just walking into the place. He glanced at Madison, who held herself tightly as they walked toward her foster mother's room. She hadn't said much to him since his outburst earlier, and as much as he wanted to regret what he'd almost said, he couldn't. Not when she was driving him away as often as she pulled him close.

Maybe once this situation with her foster brother was resolved in court, she'd settle and trust Alex more, but for now, he was still busting his ass without knowing how much she really believed in *them*.

"Ms. Evans?" A nurse approached them before they reached the room.

"Hi, Katie. And I told you to please call me Madison."

The younger woman smiled. "Madison. I'm sorry you had to get that phone call earlier."

"Were you here when Eric came by?"

The other woman nodded. "He was badgering Mrs. Grayson about you," she said, lowering her voice. "He wanted to know how she could put you in charge instead of her own flesh and blood, and then he began yelling." She paused and glanced over her shoulder. "My supervisor doesn't like when we gossip," she explained.

Madison met Alex's gaze before turning back to

Katie. "Thank you. I appreciate you being honest. I'm going to talk to my lawyer and see what I can do to keep him from bothering her again. Although it's sad. He's her son."

The younger nurse touched Madison's shoulder in understanding.

She looked at Alex then, sudden recognition lighting her gaze. "You're … Oh my God, you're the old Tampa quarterback!" She snapped her fingers. "I'm so embarrassed I can't think of your name, but my husband's from Tampa, and I'm from Miami, and he's such a huge fan!"

Alex grinned. Sometimes he actually forgot he was famous, something that had never happened while he was still playing ball.

"Can I get your autograph?" she asked excitedly, searching her pockets for a pen and paper.

He laughed. "Don't worry. I won't leave without signing something for you."

"Thank you!" she practically squealed.

Alex glanced at Madison, who hadn't said a word since the other woman had recognized Alex. Her tight smile was obvious, at least to him, and she'd taken a noticeable step back and away.

He narrowed his gaze, realizing it was the fame thing that got to her, and he wondered why. She hadn't seemed to mind when it was Jake, the kid in the wheelchair. But her uncomfortable reaction now was obvious. And that time at the dive bar, she'd made some comment about him signing the bimbo's breasts.

Before he could follow his thoughts further, Madison spoke. "I'm going to go into Franny's room," she said aloud.

Alex cleared his throat. "I'm coming with you."

"She's still sedated, so don't expect much today, okay?" Katie said to Madison. To Alex, she whispered, "I'll go find paper and pen." Her mind was obviously still on getting his autograph.

Madison pushed through the closed door, quietly walking into the room. Alex took in the cheery yellow walls and the floral hanging prints before his gaze came to a halt on a frail woman sleeping in bed.

"Just a little over a month ago, we were having full conversations," Madison said softly before stepping inside.

"I'm sure if you talk to her, she'll find it soothing, whether or not you think she can hear you. She's sedated right now. Maybe next time you see her, she'll be lucid and having a good day."

She nodded. "I hope you're right."

Even if he wasn't sure, he knew giving Madison hope couldn't hurt. "Talk to her," he said. If anyone needed to express herself, it was Madison.

"Hi, Franny," she said, pulling a chair up to the

bed. "It's Madison. I brought a friend with me today."

Alex placed a hand on Madison's shoulder.

"His name is Alex. I told you and Daniel about him a while ago, remember?"

To Alex's surprise, the older woman opened her eyes and blinked.

"Franny?" Madison said.

"Gracie?" the older woman croaked.

Madison sighed. "That's her sister. She passed away," she explained to Alex.

"No, it's Madison," she said, her voice sad.

"I'm thirsty," Franny said.

"I'll go get the nurse," Alex said, leaving the room and returning a few minutes later with a nurse who held a pitcher of water and a cup with a straw.

Before he'd walked into the room again, he'd placed a call to Jonathan and filled him in on what had transpired this morning. The lawyer had promised to do what he could to get an emergency hearing on Monday. He had a judge or two who owed him a favor and would move him up on the docket.

As Alex reentered the room, the nurse was helping Franny to a sitting position and helped her take a sip of water.

"She doesn't know me today," Madison murmured.

"It's probably the sedative we had to give her. You

can try again later or tomorrow," the nurse suggested.

Madison nodded and rose to her feet. "We should get going. Franny, I'm going to make sure you're not bothered here," she said, leaning in and giving the unresponsive woman a hug.

Alex's heart broke for both this woman who was missing out on her life and for Madison, who had again lost someone important. No wonder she was afraid to really trust.

They stepped into the hall and walked to the elevator. Alex waited until they were alone in the enclosed space and hit the pause button.

"Alex!"

"Two minutes." He backed her against the wall, holding her in place with his body.

"I hardly think this is the time or place for—"

"It's exactly the right time," he said, lifting her chin and sealing his lips over hers.

He kissed her firmly, using his tongue and all his coaxing skills until, with a resigned moan, she gave in and wrapped her arms around him and kissed him back. He urged his tongue between her lips and made love to her mouth, thrusting his tongue in and out, rubbing it against hers, mimicking the movement with his lower body rocking against hers.

It took all his willpower to ease back, but he managed, looking deep into her now-glazed eyes.

"What was that for?" she asked, running her tongue over her moist lips.

"That was to remind you that you aren't alone. You have me. And no matter how hard you try to push me away, I'm going to be right here pushing back."

She swallowed hard. "Until you're not."

He narrowed his gaze. "One of these days, I'm going to put you over my knee and give you a good spanking," he muttered.

"Alex! Wake up. You're going to test, they're going to love you, and you're going to take the job. Whether it's weekends or football season only ... you're going to be back in the spotlight."

"So?" he asked, frustrated, not getting the problem.

"So maybe you don't remember yourself when you were a star, but I do. And I'm realistic enough to know that you loved that life. The only reason you're with me now is because that didn't work out for you. When the fame returns, so will the willing women. In droves. So forgive me if I keep a level head and make sure I can still pull myself together when you decide you've had enough of me this time!"

Without warning, a male voice sounded through the elevator speaker. "Is everything okay in there?"

"Yes, sorry." She pulled out the red button on the

wall, and the elevator began its descent once more. "We hit the stop button by mistake," Madison said in a shaky voice.

Alex wasn't feeling any steadier as the pieces of the puzzle she'd been presenting since he'd gotten the job offer fell into place. He should have seen it sooner. Madison was uncomfortable with the *women* who paid attention to him. To him, they were the perks of fame he'd loved as an up-and-coming star quarterback and ones he'd taken advantage of more times than he wanted to admit. And though he no longer encouraged them, when he looked back at the man he'd been before his injury, he recalled how he sure hadn't pushed those women away when he'd been with Madison in the past.

She ran five steps ahead of him to the car, and he let her go. He knew better than to think words could convince her he really had changed for good. Like everything else with Madison, it would take time. And infinite patience.

Unless he didn't take the job. He could stick with the Thunder and the work he was doing there and give up on the idea of television and broadcasting altogether. And be the pitiful face of how to walk away from a career gracefully? he thought with more than a little disgust.

He loved the work they were doing with the organization, and if he could manage to do both things, he'd stay on here. But he was honest enough to admit that the thought of returning to football in some sort of public capacity appealed to him. He couldn't give that up, even for Madison. He had to believe that wasn't what she'd want him to do either.

He knew he was a different man now, and no amount of time in front of the camera would change that. It was her turn to change, he thought, with no small amount of frustration.

But he didn't know if she could alter a lifetime of ingrained negative expectations. And he didn't know where that would leave them if she couldn't.

TEN

Alex arrived at the rooftop bar where Riley had suggested they meet to talk. He was surprised she'd pick a bar, given her pregnant state, but it worked for him. The fact that she'd still come when he called meant a lot to him. There was no one else he could talk to about his problems with Madison besides the one woman who knew her almost as well as he did.

He ordered a Patron Reposado, in the mood for something other than scotch tonight, and though he'd assumed Riley would drink an iced tea, he figured he'd wait till she chose herself. Her pregnancy hormones had her eating all sorts of weird shit.

Someone slid into the seat beside him. Not Riley. He glanced at the man and swore. "Really? You?"

Ian shrugged and grinned. "I feel the same way. But my wife can't be in two places at once. Believe it or not, she thought I could handle you better than I could Madison."

He wasn't surprised Madison had called Riley too.

"Okay then. A Glenlivet for my ... brother," Alex said to the bartender.

He glanced at Ian, daring him to argue or throw in the word *half*, but he didn't. "I get why you walked out on Riley after she landed herself in the hospital," Alex admitted as the guy behind the bar slid a tumbler toward Ian.

His brother took a long sip. "Can't say it was one of my finer moments. Looking back, I don't think it was the right way to handle things."

Alex raised an eyebrow. "What would've worked better?" They both knew Riley had been as stubborn in her own beliefs as Madison now was in hers.

"I should have cuffed her to the bed until she saw reason." Ian lifted his glass. "A little dominance once in a while doesn't hurt."

Alex shook his head and grinned. "Probably more than I want to know about your relationship, but I get your point." He swallowed a gulp, closing his eyes at the soothing burn. "I threatened to take her over my knee," he muttered.

Ian shrugged. "So do it."

The other man clearly wasn't kidding. Alex was definitely considering it. That was a boundary they hadn't crossed, not that he wasn't tempted. Not to cause her pain but to give her pleasure.

He cleared his throat. "I need to run something

else by you," he said, figuring it was the right thing to do.

"Go on."

He went on to outline Rachel's offer, the lack of details, and the potential conflict with his current job.

"And that explains why Madison called Riley in a panic. She thinks you're going to end up moving to what? East Coast? West?"

Alex shrugged. "Even if I lived here full time, she's got other issues that need to be worked out. As for east or west…"

He shrugged. "Testing in New York this week. I'll find out more then. I don't think the move is something she's even considering as the problem. I'd assume it's a part-time gig anyway. Just during the season. At the very least, I could commute. Hell, if it meant full time, I don't think I'd take it. Believe it or not, I like being nearby the family."

"I suppose they all can grow on you," Ian conceded.

Alex shook his head at his brother's attitude. This was Ian softening, he thought wryly, and spun his drink between his palms. "Look, I don't want you to think I'm taking my current job lightly. I wouldn't bail on you or leave you and Madison in a lurch."

"I know that," Ian said, surprising Alex.

"You do?"

Ian leveled him with a long stare that reminded Alex of their father at his sternest. "Do you really think I hired you just because Riley begged me to?" The edge of his mouth curled up in a smirk.

"That's a trick question. On the one hand, yeah. She's got you wrapped." He raised his middle finger and wiggled it around.

"Nice," Ian muttered.

"On the other hand, no. You're a shrewd businessman. You do what you think is best for the company."

Ian lifted his drink in agreement.

"However, you do like to keep your woman happy."

"I hired you because I knew your work ethic from watching you with the Breakers. I know if you leave, you'll make sure things here are smooth first."

"So you wouldn't hold it against me?" He leaned against the polished wood counter.

Ian shook his head. "I wouldn't begrudge you an opportunity. I'm not that big of an ass. But I did want to discuss the PR campaign you shot down so quickly."

Alex's cheeks burned at the mention of the embarrassing photograph and billboard. "Tell me you'd let them plaster you all over at your lowest, weakest point?"

Ian drummed his fingers on the counter. "I think I'd look at it from a different angle. Or maybe I'd need someone to tell me to do it."

Alex gestured for another drink. "I'm listening."

"You're a known name. People liked watching you play. They recognize your talent."

Alex stared, having a hard time reconciling the man shooting him compliments with the one who couldn't be bothered to acknowledge him a short while ago.

"Anyone with half a brain knows it took guts to walk away before you became a vegetable or paraplegic from another hit to the head or the wrong vertebra."

A wave of nausea overtook him with the blunt description of the choice he'd faced.

"My point is," Ian went on, unaware, "parents and kids look up to you."

Alex's mind immediately went to Jake in the wheelchair.

"I believe you can change lives by allowing people to see you then and now. So what if you were knocked down? You got back up, right?" Ian shrugged and slugged down the end of his drink.

"I get it but—"

"I heard how you charmed the kid in the hotel," Ian said. "Madison told Riley you called your publicist and had them send you a picture and a jersey with your number on it so you could personally sign and send them to a teenager in a wheelchair."

Alex swallowed hard and looked away. He didn't do those things for acknowledgment.

"Imagine the good you can do for other players and injured kids whose coaches are pressuring them to play or to sign pro before they graduate college. You're a role model, if you want to be." Ian slammed his glass on the table. "By the way, nobody said it's full time or nothing on our end. Let me know if you want to take the TV gig, and we can make this work too."

"I don't know what to say." This wasn't the Ian Dare that Alex hadn't gotten to know for all those years. This was a different man. One who was treating him with respect. Almost like a family member.

Ian rose. He slid his hand into his pocket, but Alex shook his head.

"That's twice. Next one's on me then," Ian insisted.

"Quit counting."

"If we're through here, I am going to get home to my wife."

"You're assuming Madison's finished with her."

"I'm picking Riley up on my way home." Ian grinned. "She's finished when I say she is."

Alex rose to his feet. He'd already given his credit card, so their tab was settled. "I'm going to head to my place. I think Madison and I could use some space from each other. She needs to get her head on straight and decide what she wants. This push-pull is killing me," he muttered.

"She can't help it. And until she can, you need to decide if you can stick it out with her, because I can tell you that if you bail this time, you're not going to get another shot."

His gut cramped at the thought. "Yeah. I'm not going anywhere. Just giving her a night to think. Tomorrow's the hearing about her foster mother's care and holdings. I'll be there."

Ian nodded. "We all do what we have to do. Riley came around," he said, his expression suddenly showing the pain he'd been through during that time. Just as quickly, he regained his usual stoic composure. "Keep me posted on things."

"Will do."

"And if you want to run things by someone…" He left the rest unsaid, but Alex heard the unspoken offer.

"I just might do that," he said, grateful he'd been given a shot at something more than working for his half brother.

Now if Madison would just give him the same opening, maybe he could prove himself worthy of her trust as well.

* * *

Madison hadn't slept well, not that she'd expected to. She'd grown accustomed to Alex and his big body huddled around hers. Whether in her queen-sized bed or his king, they slept wrapped together. Yet she understood his need for a night apart. In truth, she'd needed it too. But last night, alone in her empty bed, she'd tossed and turned. Unfortunately, she couldn't resolve anything in her mind, not when so much in Alex's life was open-ended and uncertain. As far as she was concerned, right now it wasn't about trust, it was about facts and seeing how things played out for him. And where.

The trust thing she would have to come to terms with later.

This morning, she needed to focus on the hearing ahead of her. Alex called and insisted he'd pick her up. Not wanting to face this alone and grateful for his support, she agreed to wait for him to get her.

He rang the bell before she could grab her purse and meet him at the car, pulling her in for a kiss before either of them could speak. It didn't matter where they differed, right now they were a united front, and for that she was grateful.

"Are you ready for this?" he asked as they walked toward the courtroom.

She nodded. "I have nothing to hide."

He held open the heavy wooden door to the courtroom, and she stepped inside. He clasped her hand on the walk down the aisle. Eric and his attorney hadn't yet arrived, but Jonathan waited for her at the table. Alex took a seat directly behind her.

He squeezed her shoulder just as Eric and his attorney walked in. She had to give it to her foster brother, he cleaned up well, wearing a gray pinstriped suit and red tie. He might have passed for a banker, the way he'd slicked his hair back and held himself with an air of authority and confidence. But it was the Visine bottle he pulled out of his jacket pocket so he could add drops to his eyes that gave him away, at least in Madison's mind.

"Remember," Jonathan said, redirecting her attention. "When you're up there, you answer only if his attorney asks you a direct question. Inflammatory upsetting statements? Ignore them," he instructed her in a lawyerly voice, but his eyes held a glint of empathy. He'd seen her history. They both knew today wouldn't be pretty.

The only good thing was that Alex hadn't been with her when she and Jonathan had gone over testimony. Jonathan had wanted her alone and able to concentrate on his instructions, and she'd been grateful. A part of her wished Alex wasn't here today, but there was no stopping him, and she hadn't bothered to try.

She glanced toward the other table, where Eric and his attorney sat conferring the same way Madison and Jonathan just had. Eric glanced up, met her gaze, and shot her a direct glare mere seconds before the judge and his court clerk and deputy walked into the room. The next minutes passed in a blur of formalities handled by the lawyers.

Of course it was up to her foster brother to prove his case, which meant he paraded witnesses attesting to his close relationship with his mother, his stellar character—before he began an attempt to assassinate hers.

People Madison hadn't seen in years came before the judge. Her first foster mother claimed she'd stolen personal things from the house and she'd had to send Madison back. More like she'd pawned the items in an attempt to pay for the alcohol addiction she hid from her husband and the state. Even at twelve years old, Madison had been familiar with the signs. From there, her case worker from years ago, aged and gray now, took the stand, elaborating reasons Madison hadn't lasted at each foster home.

Nausea filled her at the unfairness of it all. The truth was, as Jon did his best to counter, the woman couldn't possibly remember Madison with all the other kids in and out of the system over the years. She was relying on a folder of printed information that included none of the underlying circumstances or Madison's truths.

As a social worker herself, she understood how little time most put into keeping up-to-date records. She'd struggled day and night to keep up with the caseload when she'd worked with abused women, and paperwork was done in between visits with victims. More than once, Jonathan rose and objected to the other lawyer's insinuations or attempts to discredit Madison, questioning the reasons for the character assassination. He offered an excuse of laying ground-work, and the judge agreed to humor him a little while longer.

The morning marched on with more of the same, and Madison was beyond embarrassed that Alex had to hear her sordid youth, which she never discussed and preferred not to remember.

"Your Honor!" Jonathan rose again, his voice filled with frustration. "Is there a point to this? It's up to Mr. Grayson to prove his claims that Ms. Evans used undue influence to gain access to her foster mother's power of attorney. So far I've heard nothing of the sort."

"Good point, Mr. Ridgeway." His Honor, Judge Collins, a kindly looking, balding older man, turned to Eric's attorney. "Mr. Newcomb?"

"Just laying the foundation, Your Honor," he repeated in a sickeningly placating tone. "But we're happy to move on. We'd like to call Madison Evans to the stand."

Her stomach cramped, but she'd been prepped for this moment, something Jonathan leaned close and reminded her. Alex placed a soothing hand on her shoulder, but she couldn't focus on him now. She couldn't even look at him.

Rising, she walked to the small witness box and took her seat.

Alex took in the stiff set of Madison's shoulders and the way she wouldn't glance his way or meet his gaze so he could offer reassurance. He leaned forward in his seat, every muscle in his body tense and prepared to strike. Not that he could do a damned thing but sit and watch. There was nothing he hated more than feeling utterly useless when she needed him.

More than once this morning, he regretted not putting his personal feelings aside and staying with her last night. Once more in his life, he'd let ego get in the way of common, rational sense.

After some preliminary easy questions, her step-brother's lawyer went for stabbingly painful questions. "How many foster homes were you in, Ms. Evans?"

"Five or six."

"Actually, it was seven."

"It's not something I like to remember."

"No, I suppose not, given that nobody wanted to keep you."

"Your Honor," Jonathan said, rising.

They'd been advised that since this was a hearing and not a trial, formal objections wouldn't apply.

"Move it along, Mr. Newcomb. All this has already been established and is in the records."

The other lawyer nodded. "Then you ended up with the Graysons, and things changed for you."

Since it wasn't a question, Madison didn't answer. Good girl, Alex thought.

"Were you told why the Graysons, who were an unusual type of foster family in that they didn't need the money provided by the state for your care, wanted to take you in?"

Madison nodded. "Franny couldn't have kids after Eric, and she'd always wanted a daughter."

"And they had money," the bastard lawyer said.

Again, no question, and Madison merely stared at him.

"Were you and Mrs. Grayson close?" he asked.

"Yes."

"She took you shopping, bought you clothes?"

"Yes."

He rested an elbow on the witness stand. "And you had your own room, unlike your last six ... no, make that seven foster homes, correct?"

"Yes."

Alex saw the tension, the toll this was taking on her. His hands were fists at his sides.

"Had you brought any clothes with you from the home before?" the man asked.

"A few."

"Personal things?" he clipped out.

"I didn't have any," she said softly, her jaw trembling along with her voice.

Alex gripped the stainless bar that separated him from Jonathan, leaned forward, and whispered, "Do something or I will."

"Shh. I can't and you know it. This has to play out."

Alex bit the inside of his cheek, his jaw aching from the effort of clenching his teeth to keep quiet.

"Is there a problem, Mr. Ridgeway?" the judge asked.

Jonathan partially rose. "No, Your Honor." He lowered himself back into his seat.

"So after your mother took off and your father abandoned you in a shopping mall," the other attorney asked as he paced in front of Madison, "after seven unsuccessful foster placements, you landed with the Graysons. In a big house in a wealthy neighborhood, in the best school district for miles. You were bought new clothes, given your own room… Be honest, Ms. Evans. You saw the gold pot at the end of the rainbow, didn't you? An easy target in an older woman who couldn't have more children, who wanted a daughter … You knew it would be better to suck up to her than to cause trouble like you had in your other homes, isn't that right?"

Madison's jaw worked back and forth before answering. "No. I loved Franny."

She folded her arms across her chest, a protective gesture Alex knew well. He also knew how hard it was for her to admit to those feelings, and it took all his willpower not to launch across the room and drag her into his arms and out of there.

But the lawyer wasn't finished demolishing her pride. "Mr. Grayson testified you were always spending time with his mother when you weren't in school. Sucking up to her, putting thoughts in her head as you got older about how much better you'd treat her than her own son when she got sick. From there, it wasn't difficult to assume Daniel Grayson would include you in his will. And ultimately, you gained Franny's power of attorney, where you could put her in a home, sell her house from beneath her, and put the proceeds toward a rec center."

"That Franny wanted! She wasn't interested in destroying the land with overdevelopment. Eric, you know this. You know your mother better than that."

"You lying bitch!"

Alex rose to his feet, but the judge banged the gavel hard. "Silence."

"Your Honor, there are no questions being asked here!" Jonathan said loudly.

Eric's lawyer looked at the judge, acting contrite and sorry. "I apologize. I was just trying to establish undue influence, Your Honor."

The judge rapped his gavel. "You've more than made your point."

Hopefully the judge felt sorry for Madison and understood the true dynamic of her relationship with Franny Grayson, Alex thought. It was obvious how much she'd needed a mother, even if she hadn't said as much.

But as the next group of witnesses testified, things didn't get any better. Parents of Eric's friends backed up the amount of time Franny spent with Madison, who they all agreed hadn't gone out of her way to make friends in her new school. They all said they admired Franny for taking in a difficult child but wondered why she chose her over her own son, the implication of undue influence on Madison's part clear. Said it wasn't like the other woman, who valued her blood relatives dearly.

Although the hearing was supposed to last just one

day, Eric's lawyer had drawn things out, and by the end of the day, everyone was exhausted, and it was too late for Jonathan to present Madison's witnesses to Franny's intent and state of mind. Or Jonathan's terrorizing his own mother at the nursing home.

The hearing would continue tomorrow. When, according to the message Alex played during a recess, he was scheduled to fly to New York.

* * *

By the time the long day ended, Madison's entire body trembled from exhaustion. Outside the courtroom, they parted ways with Jonathan, who promised to meet her at nine a.m. tomorrow.

Alex was quiet on the way back to her apartment, and Madison didn't have anything to say either. He stopped for food, and they ate it in silence. He allowed her the space she needed to decompress. Once again, she was amazed at how well he knew what she needed. Even last night's argument took a back seat to today's drama, and she was too wiped out to even think. He parked in a guest spot at her building, and they walked inside and up to her place.

She sat down on her bed and pulled off her heels, groaning as she stretched her feet. Alex walked past her into the bathroom, and she heard the sound of running water.

"What are you doing?" she asked as he walked out.

"Running you a hot shower so you can relax." He shot her a smile and headed for her dresser, pulling out her favorite lounging pants and camisole.

"Alex?"

"I'm serious. You need a breather. I want you to take one."

Her heart melted at his thoughtfulness. "Under one condition."

He raised his eyebrows.

"You take one with me." She didn't care what had kept them apart last night; she needed him now, and clearly he was here.

"I'm glad you asked."

They undressed in silence. Nothing erotic or sexy about her exhausted movements, she thought. And as she stepped into the shower naked along with him, the hot water streaming over them, she didn't think anything had ever felt better.

She let out a long sigh of appreciation as she tilted her face up and let the spray wash away the stress of the day. She refused to let her mind replay the embarrassment, mortification, or painful memories, concentrating instead on letting each tight muscle relax.

When his warm body wrapped around her from behind, his chest against her bare back, his thick erection between her cheeks, his arms around her waist, head on her shoulder, she melted back into him.

His hands settled on her belly, palms splayed, fingers dipping downward. "How much do you need to relax, Angel?"

His fingers trailed a path down to her thatch of hair and slid over her outer lips. "Alex," she moaned, her hips thrusting of their own accord, her clit seeking pressure he wasn't yet willing to give.

One finger on either side of her sex, he played with her, teasing, arousing her until she couldn't stand another second. "Alex, please."

"Please what?"

"Touch my clit. Make me come." She heard the plea in her voice, the whine through the thick haze of arousal.

His harsh laugh vibrated through her body, his cock hot and hard against her. "All you had to do was ask."

He shifted his wrist and captured her clit between his fingers, starting slowly, gliding his fingertip up one side and down the other. She rolled her hips in time to his movements, whimpering at the onslaught of desire peaking inside her.

"Is this what you need?" he asked, sliding a finger deep inside and curling forward, hitting her in exactly the right spot.

"Yes," she groaned, her body so very close.

In and out he pumped the long digit until the ultimate wave crashed over her. At exactly the same moment, he tweaked her clit with his free hand, and she shattered in his arms. He kept up the pressure and pumping of his hand until she rode out her orgasm and fell against him, limp and sated.

He waited until she could stand and shut off the water.

She turned and looked into his dark eyes. "That was amazing," she said in a husky voice. "Your turn." She grasped for his erection, but he stepped out of reach.

"I told you, you needed to unwind and relax. You did. Now, let's get you dry and into bed."

She was amazed at how sleepy she actually was and let him run a towel over her hair and helped dry herself off before dressing in the clothes he'd picked out. "We usually sleep naked," she said drowsily.

"And we usually have sex. If I have to lie next to your naked body, you won't get any sleep, and that's exactly what you need."

"Yeah," she said gratefully and over a yawn as she climbed beneath the blanket and cuddled into her pillow. "You're staying, right?" A part of her recognized that, had her defenses not been down, she wouldn't have asked. She couldn't bring herself to think, much less care.

"Damn right," he muttered. "I'm going to get dressed and join you." He brushed a kiss over her lips. "We'll talk in the morning," she thought she heard him say before darkness overtook her completely.

ELEVEN

Madison awoke with a jolt, looked at the clock, and realized they'd both overslept. She remembered falling asleep first, and after Alex had taken care of her, he had obviously forgotten to set the alarm.

She shook him awake. "You have to hurry or we're going to be late."

"Shit," he muttered, sitting up. The sheet draped around his waist, and his gorgeous chest greeted her, making her wish they had more time.

"Quit ogling and go shower," he said in a gruff voice.

She grinned and jumped out of bed, glad she'd woken up feeling better, with yesterday's nightmare behind her. One more day to get through.

They raced through their morning routine. She grabbed a quick shower and blow-dried her hair. When she was finished, she cracked open the bathroom door to get some cooler air while she put on a little bit of makeup.

Alex's voice sounded from the other room. "I understand it's an inconvenience, but I can't help it. Something important came up, and I need to be in town today. Remind them they called me about it at the last second yesterday, so me canceling today can't come as too much of a surprise."

She walked out of the bathroom as he ended the call. "What was that all about?" she asked, dressing for court as they talked.

He met her gaze, but his expression showed he was clearly uncomfortable. "I didn't get a chance to talk to you after the hearing yesterday. You were so tired and—"

"Just tell me," she pressed him.

"I got a message during a break in the hearing yesterday. My agent said the people in New York set up a flight and meetings for today and a test with Allison for tomorrow. I agreed because I thought the hearing would be finished, but things changed. So I postponed traveling."

A mixture of feelings assaulted her at once. Gratitude for his thoughtfulness, annoyance that the job existed at all, intruding on what would otherwise be a perfect situation between them, and then a gut cramp as the reality of what this job meant settled around her again.

"You need to go." She zipped her skirt and fussed with her blouse. "It's important, and today won't be nearly as grueling as yesterday. It's Jonathan's turn to prove our side, so Eric will be the one grilled, not me. I'll be fine." And she needed to relearn to stand on her own feet and not fall back on Alex when things went bad.

He narrowed his gaze. "I said from day one this was a *we* situation. You and me. I'm not going to leave you mid-nightmare just so I can—"

"Go test for something that could very well change your life? That means a lot to you? Don't take this the wrong way, but I don't need you there." Did she want him there? More than anything. But she wouldn't let him sacrifice his dreams for her.

"They can reschedule."

"What if they can't? Or won't? Or decide you're being difficult and go with someone else?" She picked her earring off the dresser and inserted it into her earlobe, doing the same to the other one.

He frowned at her. "You're pushing me away."

"I'm being realistic. Today will be cake for me compared to yesterday, and if you weigh things, you need to be in New York more than you need to be here."

He studied her, as if he could get inside her head and decide if she was telling the truth or saying what she thought he wanted to hear. "Alex! Call them back and go to New York."

She turned away, hoping on hope she was doing the right thing by sending him there. Her mind insisted it was best, for him and for her. They were two independent people who would either make a relationship work or not. She didn't want to be a burden to him. But her heart? Oh, that had been battered and beaten so badly over the years she couldn't imagine how things could work out for them if he became a celebrity television star with the world—and women—at his beck and call once more.

"Are you sure?" He walked up to her, grasping her forearms and forcing her to meet his gaze.

She managed a bright smile. "Absolutely. Now go make your call and let me finish getting ready so I can grab some coffee before I go to the courthouse."

He hesitated. "I don't like leaving you."

"Well, you need to go," she said.

He placed a warm kiss on her lips.

Warm but quick, and in seconds, he'd grabbed his phone and dialed, already distracted by all the possibilities the bright lights and big city had to offer.

* * *

Madison had been right about today's events at the hearing. It was Eric's turn on the stand. He looked more disheveled than he had yesterday, giving her hope his appearance would have an impact on the judge. Jonathan was brilliant in his questioning, making it clear yesterday's character assassination had been inaccurate.

Jonathan grilled him on his visit to his mother at dawn that had upset her so much, but Eric had that covered. He claimed he was a distraught son. Seeing his mother in a nursing home, knowing someone else was making decisions for her and for his family home, had all gotten to him. He sounded contrite and genuine, and he was lying through his teeth. But Jonathan had been unable to rattle him or get him to admit to needing the money from the sale of the land instead of donating it as Madison claimed Franny wanted. In the end, they'd done all they could.

Whatever way the judge decided, Madison knew she'd done her best by Franny, the same way the other woman had done for her. That's what mattered, and she could put her head on the pillow and sleep at night, knowing she'd given this fight with Eric her all.

She picked up dinner to eat at home and walked into her apartment at the end of the day, drained. She tossed her keys on the counter and poured herself a glass of white wine and ate alone before turning in for the night. It wasn't what she'd gotten used to, but it might be what she'd need to expect in the future.

Because the entire day had passed, and Alex hadn't checked in. No text, no phone call, no email.

*   *   *

Overscheduled didn't begin to cover what Alex's agent and S&E had planned from the minute he landed in New York. His agent, Kevin Falcon, sent a car for him, and the first stop was a late lunch, at which Kevin toasted his return to the big time.

The other man's enthusiasm made Alex uncomfortable. He'd been out of the spotlight for a while now and had gotten used to the quieter way of living. Kevin began by assuming the television test, which was now scheduled first thing tomorrow morning, would lead to him being offered the television show. Done deal. He had plans ready to go based on that.

Using the new job as leverage, he intended to put out feelers with big companies looking for hot sports guys for commercial ads. "Because within a month of the viral campaign I'm sure they'll launch, you'll be on everyone's lips, and women will flock to you again."

None of which had been on Alex's radar. None of which he was certain he wanted. And though he conveyed his reservations to Kevin, the other man clearly wasn't listening. He had his own agenda, which would line his pockets, and he expected Alex would give in and go along. Probably because, before his injury, he always had.

He then had a pre-dinner meeting with the head of S&E Network so the guy could schmooze with him ahead of the screen test with Allison Edwards. Alex didn't have the opportunity to get to know or assess the other man, as Kevin was up his ass the entire time, as if he was afraid Alex would up and disappear on him before tomorrow.

And from there, his agent drove him over to the newest hot spot to *see and be seen* in town, so he could meet Allison for dinner and warm up to her before their on-air pairing test. For this meeting, Kevin decided to make himself scarce. Alex didn't understand the man except that greed was his sole motivation. All the years before, he'd never cared as long as the other man did his job. Today he saw Kevin more clearly and wasn't comfortable with his selfish, shark-like qualities.

"Make sure you get the chemistry flowing," Kevin said as his parting shot before dropping Alex off at the restaurant and assuring him the limo would be waiting for him on his return.

The only good news in the entire day was that Rachel wasn't anywhere to be seen. Apparently she'd been used as the connection to Alex and that was it. Something he was grateful for. He was glad to have made peace with her and his past, but he certainly didn't want her anywhere near him in the future.

The restaurant, a place aptly named Buzz, was hopping with people, many of them famous. He caught sight of Eli Manning, the New York Giants quarterback, and his wife, and stopped to talk for a while. Eli was a guy Alex admired. Whereas while playing, he'd thought the man with his one woman was too tame, Alex now envied the home life the guy had and the way he managed his career. A few choice commercial spots, specific charity events, and time home with his family in between playing. Man, Alex realized now how screwed up his priorities had been before his injury. If his agent had his way, he'd be thrown right back into that fast-track way of life.

He ran his hand through his hair and groaned as he was hit by the sudden need to hear Madison's voice. He hadn't spoken to her the entire day. Hell, he hadn't had five minutes to breathe or even think for himself.

He pulled his phone from his pants pocket and began to dial just as the hostess came over. "Mr. Dare? Your dinner companion has arrived. May I show you to your table?"

Resigned, he slid his cell back into his pocket and followed the woman over to where Allison Edwards sat waiting.

"Alex!" she said, rising as he walked over.

"Hi, Allison." He leaned in and kissed her cheek. They'd met once or twice at various functions, and she'd interviewed him after a playoff game.

The good news was he'd been smart enough not to hit on women he worked with in a professional capacity—before Madison, that is—and he could have a decent working relationship with Allison, should he want to go that route.

Alex had to admit he and Allison got along well. They had a lot in common, with their love and knowledge of sports. They were able to find a rhythm and banter without trying too hard, and he wasn't at all concerned about them having an issue on camera in the morning. Over dinner, they shared a bottle of wine—not his usual choice of drink, but she'd insisted he try her new favorite, and he had to admit it was good.

As the evening wore on, the restaurant grew more crowded, and it became difficult to hear each other speak. She moved from across the table to the seat beside his, enabling her to lean close while they talked. By the time the waiter asked if they wanted dessert, Alex was ready to crash in his bed, but Allison ordered chocolate mousse, and he had no choice but to wait. He asked for a double espresso, hoping the shot of caffeine would help him stay awake for a little while longer.

The waiter brought the small dessert with two spoons. Alex shook his head and declined her offer to share. But she tasted and moaned about how good it was, offering him a taste with her spoon. He wasn't the least bit tempted, not in the chocolate treat or in her, as he belatedly realized she was also putting herself on the menu.

He shook his head and swore to himself, wondering when he'd gotten so out of practice that he didn't notice a beautiful woman coming on to him. "Allison, listen. I'm involved with someone."

She leaned back in her seat and watched him, amusement in her dark eyes. "All the good ones usually are."

"I'm sorry." He didn't know what else to say.

She flipped her long hair behind her and laughed. "Alex, come on. You haven't been out of the game for that long."

Completely lost, he shook his head. "Maybe I have. What's going on?"

"The offer is a done deal. Tomorrow is just a formality for the network brass. And this?" She gestured between them. "You and me? Dinner? The choice of restaurants, the new hot spot where we're sure to be seen, all carefully orchestrated for exactly that. To *be seen*. The two new hosts of the hottest new sports show. Tomorrow at the *audition*, they'll get some damn good, comfortable clips to use for promotion."

He narrowed his gaze, but she went on, and he figured the best thing he could do was let her explain. Because he felt like he'd dropped onto another planet.

"And once the clips are released, everyone will be speculating whether that chemistry between us on the air is so good because we're a couple off the air too. Backed up by pictures of us here. Tonight." She waved a hand around them, and suddenly everything became clear.

"Kevin set this up." His SOB agent, Alex thought.

"Well, Kevin and the network. Come on, it's brilliant! Your stock and cachet will only go up when we explode onto the scene. They're going to take this show national and run it on TV as well as the Internet," she said, her enthusiasm and excitement huge.

"Did anyone even think of just asking me to go along?" he asked through clenched teeth. Because no way in hell would he have said yes.

She wrinkled her nose. "Well, your agent said you were waffling about wanting the job. He figured you just needed a good push and a reminder of all you've been missing out on to get your head back into the game. So to speak."

"He had no right to lie to me."

"Part of the reason was to make things between us seem natural. If you knew someone would be shooting cell phone pictures tonight for gossip rags, would you have been as relaxed with me? I was an actress before the news gig."

"Incredible." He rubbed a hand over his face. "Did you or my genius agent, or even the network executives, ever hear of the concept of free will?" he asked, rising from his seat. "You can set up all the press and fake publicity you want, but it won't make it real. You can't make me want to take this job."

He'd been counting on the test to see how he felt in front of the camera. He'd needed to hear the concept for the show, to know what kind of commute it'd entail. But nobody had laid out details for him yet. And he'd been taken in by his own agent, someone he ought to be able to trust.

"You can't say you don't want it," Allison said. "Or that you wouldn't be great doing it."

"None of that matters when I can't trust the people around me." He stormed away from the table, pausing at the front to take care of the bill. Afterwards, he headed back to his hotel, furious and frustrated.

What a bust the entire day had been. And by the time he finally ended up in his hotel room, it was close to midnight, and he couldn't call Madison because, after the day she'd probably had, she would be fast asleep.

*   *   *

Madison arrived at work in the morning, her mood down and foul. Not hearing from Alex had her on edge, and it took everything inside her to think positively and not jump to the worst possible conclusions. If this relationship was going to work, she needed to learn how to trust.

She walked into the office and immediately headed for the break room, needing coffee to keep herself running this morning. As soon as she entered the small room, conversation stopped.

Madison glanced at the two women she recognized as secretaries for the PR people. "Hi," Madison said. "I don't mean to interrupt. I'm just going to get coffee, and I'll let you get back to your conversation."

"Have you seen the sports blogs this morning?" Gail, one of the women, asked Madison.

Madison shook her head. "No. Is there something good in them?" She added milk and one sugar packet to her coffee, stirring as she asked.

"Yes, actually," the other woman said.

"Madison!" Riley came running into the room, interrupting the conversation. "I've been looking all over for you. We need to talk."

Madison turned to her friend. "Sure. I just want to see what has them so interested," she said, gesturing to the other women.

Riley shot them a glare Madison didn't understand.

"Later. What I have to say is urgent," she said, grasping Madison's hand and pulling her out of the room.

"What's wrong?" she asked Riley, digging her heels into the carpet, concerned.

"Not here. Come on. Let's go into your office." Riley began pulling her once more.

"You're scaring me," Madison muttered, letting her friend drag her into the room, where she shut the door and locked it behind them. "Riley—"

"Okay, sit. And listen. There's something in the morning gossip columns that you need to see. But you need to let me show you, and you need to not jump to conclusions, no matter how bad things *look*."

Her stomach flipped over, and she lowered herself into her chair. "He hasn't been in touch."

"What?" Riley pulled a chair close to her and sat down.

"Alex. That's what you want to show me, right? There's something about him in the blogs? It makes sense. Because since he left, I haven't heard from him. Not once."

Riley clasped their hands together, but Madison was numb inside and out and barely felt her friend's touch. "There is an explanation. I'm sure."

"Just show me. Is it in Behind the Bleachers with Ben?" Madison asked of the infamous website.

Riley nodded.

Madison turned and hit a button to bring her computer to life. She typed in the sports blog that was standard for everyone in the sports world to read. Sometimes Ben hit it head on, and other times, he missed the mark completely. But there was no doubt the man had reach.

The blog came onto the screen along with a set of photographs. Alex and a beautiful blonde Madison recognized as Allison Edwards, the woman he was to screen-test with. In one shot, they were laughing across from one another. In another photo, they were side by side, heads together, obviously talking intimately. And in the third picture, Allison held out her spoon, and Alex's mouth was open and waiting.

Pain gripped her heart. "Well, that explains the silence."

"No. Listen to me. I used to work in PR, and I know not everything is what it seems."

She managed a smile. "I know you're right. But even if it's perfectly innocent, I don't know that I can deal with this part of his life." Looking at the photos made her nauseous. Not hearing from him left her mind spinning and creating all sorts of awful possibilities.

"Why don't you take the day off," Riley suggested. "You've had a rough couple of days. Plus the judge is due to rule soon, and you'd have to leave anyway."

Normally Madison would argue, but not today. "Thanks. I think I'll do that."

They rose, and Riley pulled Madison into a hug. "I'll call you later and check in."

"Thanks," she whispered, not wanting to give in to the overwhelming emotions swamping her and cry.

She packed up her bag and headed home, her thoughts on Alex and all the reasons she couldn't deal with this part of his life. Even if those photographs were deliberately misleading, it didn't change what was broken inside of Madison. Yes, Alex had proven himself to her over and over, but her insecurities and issues were real and deep-seated enough that she couldn't imagine living with those feelings of abandonment being brought up over and over again.

* * *

Alex woke up at three, having booked the earliest flight he could manage out of New York the night before. He'd paid a premium, but he didn't care. He arrived at the airport in Miami and immediately took a cab straight to the stadium.

He'd never been so wired in his life. He'd barely gotten any sleep last night, and taking a six a.m. flight meant he still hadn't called Madison.

He strode through the hallway leading to his office,

needing one thing and one thing only. To see Madison. Everything else could wait.

Riley barreled out of her office, stopping in front him. "You. Me. Talk. Now."

"No. I need to see Madison."

"She's not here. She left early."

He blew out a long breath. "She's supposed to be working today. Did something happen with her foster mother or the hearing?"

"Now you're concerned? Where the hell were you all day and night yesterday?" Riley asked, raising her voice. "Oh, I'm sorry. Snuggling up with your new costar at some new hip place in Manhattan. Too busy to call your girlfriend and check in."

He set his jaw. "Fucking pictures," he muttered. "I wanted to get to her first."

"Did you ever think to try the phone?"

"My flight this morning was at six, and I didn't get back in last night until almost midnight."

Riley blew out a long breath. "You blew it, buddy."

"Don't tell me she believes what those pictures imply." He'd been laying the groundwork between them for months now. And though she'd admitted to worrying about him returning to old habits, no way could she believe it would happen in just twenty-four hours.

Riley blew out a long breath. "I don't think she

does."

Relief swept through him. "Thank God."

"But that doesn't mean she can handle what comes along with the famous *you*."

He rubbed a hand over his face. "I love her."

Riley's expression lit up her entire face. "I knew it! Have you told her?"

"Not exactly but—"

"Then what are you doing here talking to me? Go home and use your words." She grinned at him like a crazy woman.

Who'd have thought his love life was so important to her?

"Have you been reading those how-to books on raising kids?" he asked.

Her blush gave her away, and he laughed.

"What? I couldn't handle *What to Expect When You're Expecting*." She wrinkled her nose. "Too many gross details nobody wants to know ahead of time."

He shook his head and groaned. "Go torture your husband, will you? I have to get home." He started for the elevator when Riley called his name, and he turned back.

"Madison just sent me a text. Judge has made his decision. She's meeting her lawyer at the courthouse."

TWELVE

Alex arrived at the courthouse too late to hear the judge's decision. He walked through the double doors and found Jonathan gathering his papers and checking his messages.

"What'd I miss? And where is Madison?" he asked his friend.

Jonathan glanced up from his cell, looking Alex up and down. "You look like shit."

"Nice. Thank you. I took an early flight from New York this morning. I haven't had much sleep." Not to mention, he'd been driving in circles trying to find Madison. "Now what happened here?"

"I can't believe it, but we lost."

"What?" Alex braced a hand on the tabletop.

"The judge said there wasn't enough evidence to show undue influence; however, he felt that since Franny's dementia signs started before she signed the power of attorney and living will, he should err on the side of the biological child."

"Son of a bitch." Alex could only imagine the pain Madison was experiencing. "How did she take it?"

Jonathan met his gaze. "Not well. I mean, she seemed off from the minute she got here, and the judge's decision didn't help. Add to that, as he was leaving, her bastard foster brother threatened to get a restraining order to keep her away from his mother."

Alex closed his eyes and groaned.

"I don't think he could swing that. He didn't prove anything against Madison in this hearing except that she wasn't related by blood. Anyway, she said she needed to be alone and took off."

Could this day go any more wrong? Alex wondered. "Thanks, man. I know you did the best you could." He slapped his friend on the back.

Jonathan picked up his briefcase. "I'm just sorry it fell short."

"Me too."

Alex headed out to his car and started the engine, needing the air conditioning so he could think more clearly. Where would Madison go if she were upset? Right now, she was feeling abandoned by him, let down by the court, and rejected by her foster brother.

He called Riley only to find out she hadn't heard from her at all. "She lost the hearing. I'm going to check her place. If you hear from her in between, call me."

He disconnected the call.

He arrived at her apartment to find her car wasn't in its spot and she wasn't home. Instead of leaving, he settled in to wait.

* * *

Madison drove aimlessly, still in disbelief over the ruling. She'd always believed Franny's wishes would be upheld. That the judge had decided blood was thicker really hurt. Doing her best no longer felt like it was enough.

Suddenly, her phone buzzed. A quick glance confirmed it was Alex. But she wasn't ready to talk to him. She didn't know what she wanted to say. She also didn't want to go home to her empty apartment and dwell on the last twenty-four hours.

She headed out of Miami and drove toward the suburbs, her destination not clear until she turned onto an old residential street, realizing she'd driven to the neighborhood where she'd lived with her parents. The houses were as rundown as she remembered from her young mind. Overgrown grass and weeds covered most of the lawns. Few were green, and sadly, most had turned brown from neglect and lack of care.

She stopped in front of the house where she'd grown up, trying to remember any good memories before her mother had left and her father had abandoned her, but none came. Before melancholy could overwhelm her completely, she put her car in drive.

A little while later, she'd driven past one or two other foster homes, skipping Franny's in favor of visiting the older woman in person. If Eric followed through on his threat to get a restraining order, this might be the last time she could see her. Although Jonathan assured her he wouldn't win, she was past believing in anyone or anything.

And wasn't that pathetic, she thought. Ignoring the voice in her head asking if that was how she really wanted to live the rest of her life, doubting and skeptical, she walked into the nursing home, grateful when nobody stopped her on the way to Franny's room.

She knocked and was heartened by the loud *come in* she received in response.

"Franny?" Madison asked, pushing the door open.

"Gracie!" Franny said, excitement in her voice. Madison's stomach plummeted along with her hopes.

Madison walked over and kissed the older woman's cheek.

"You look wonderful today."

The nurses here took good care of her. Madison made certain to stop by at unexpected times and days, to make sure nothing she saw was for a visitor's benefit.

"Thanks. So do you." Franny giggled a bit, making Madison think she was in an earlier age.

"I took a walk in the garden today. I was hoping that good-looking man, Daniel, would come by."

Madison's heart clenched. "Did he?"

Franny shook her head. "Not today, so I played cards with some friends after lunch."

"A good day then?"

"So far."

Madison smiled because, in Franny's mind, that's all that counted. And maybe that should count for Madison too. Franny wasn't unhappy now.

"What about you? Where's that handsome man you've been telling me about? Aren't you going to bring him to visit?"

Madison decided to play along as if she were Gracie, answering with her own life's truths.

"Last time I brought him, you were asleep. I'll try to bring him by again, but he's interviewing for a new job, and I'm not sure if that'll take him out of town or not."

Franny frowned. "You sound sad about that."

"Do I?" Madison sighed. "I'm a little torn about it." Feeling a bit weird since Franny didn't really comprehend, Madison still explained what her history really had been with Alex and brought her up to date with the situation now.

Franny patted the edge of the bed, and Madison settled in beside her. "Madison, honey, do you love him?"

Madison's gaze swung to Franny's. She was here. And this might be the last chance she ever had to talk to her. She swallowed hard, nodding. "I tried really hard not to love him, but I do."

"You can't keep running from love just because you're afraid of being left behind, right?"

Madison shook her head. "Wow, when you have a good day, you really go for the jugular."

"I have to say what's important when I can."

"Yeah." She understood, and the lump formed again in her throat. The doctor had said to cherish these precious moments.

"Look, we both know that by the time you came to us, you'd been in and out of so many homes, you didn't want to count on anyone."

Madison looked down at her lap rather than into her foster mom's bright green eyes.

"It took me a year to win you over and get you to believe I wasn't going to turn my back on you. Ever."

Tears sprang to Madison's eyes because, with this damned disease, that's exactly what she felt like Franny was doing to her. The rational part of Madison knew the memory lapses weren't within Franny's control, but the little girl in her felt abandoned all over again.

"I know, honey. I know," Franny said, obviously reading her mind. "But I will always love you, even if I can't say it or if I don't recognize you."

Madison managed a nod. Then, because she owed it to her, she told Franny the rest of the truth. "Eric took me to court over your power of attorney and health care proxy. I hired the best attorney I could, but the judge ruled in his favor. He's going to sell the house so they can build condominiums. And he's going to try to keep me from seeing you."

Franny blew out a long breath. "He's got a mean streak. You can't let him stop you from seeing your man, Gracie. You know that, right?"

And just like that, it was over. Madison teared up all over again.

"I know." She managed to pull herself together and decided to say everything she would have said to a lucid Franny. "I would do it all again to help you the way you helped me. I did everything I could for you."

Franny clasped her hand and began to hum a tune Madison didn't recognize. "Remember that song? We'd sing it when I was waiting for Daniel and you were waiting for your man. Are you waiting for him now?"

"I don't know. Maybe I'll go see where he is," Madison said.

"That's a good idea."

Madison looked at Franny. "Thank you for everything. But most of all, thank you for being the only real mother I ever had," she said, pulling the frail woman into a long hug.

"That's my girl," she thought she heard Franny whisper.

Or maybe she'd imagined it. It didn't matter.

She was Franny's girl, Madison thought. From the moment the couple had taken her in, they'd treated her like their own daughter. It didn't matter what Eric thought or what the court said. She was Franny's daughter of the heart. And that was the only thing that mattered.

Madison shook her head. "I don't know if he's my man."

But she did. In her heart, where it counted, Alex was hers. Madison decided it was time to go home and deal with her real life. The one that existed in this moment.

And if that meant she had to live with whatever career choices made him happy, wasn't that a small price to pay? She didn't have to like it, but she did have to live with it. Up till now, he'd done all the changing and giving. It was her turn.

*　　*　　*

Alex was getting good and worked up, pacing Madison's apartment and glaring out the window. By the time her car pulled into her assigned parking spot, he was out of his mind worried, not knowing where she'd gone after getting the bad news, and she hadn't returned his texts or his calls.

When she put the key in the lock and walked in, he was waiting in the living room, back to the window, arms folded over his chest. "Well, it's about damned time."

"Excuse me?" She blinked, her eyes puffy and red from crying. The sight hurt, but he was still furious she'd left him hanging without a word.

"Do you have any idea how worried I was?"

She shook her head. "I thought you were calling and texting from New York, not Florida. How would I know you were home? And if anyone was left hanging, it was me. Where the hell were you for the last twenty-four hours? You didn't pick up the phone and text or call!" She tossed her keys and purse onto the table and folded her arms across her chest, mimicking his pose ... and calling him on his hypocritical bullshit.

"Madison—"

"And while we're at it, tell me why I had to see those photographs and still not hear a word from you."

"I can explain everything," he said, his heart racing

as he remembered everything between them he'd put aside during his concern for her after the hearing.

"The words of a guilty man if I ever heard them," she said, but she didn't look angry.

He was confused by her mixed signals. She strode over to him and grasped him by the shoulders. She was slight but determined as she turned and backed him over to the sofa, pushing him into the couch cushions.

"What do you think you're doing?" he asked.

"Having my say."

He narrowed his gaze. He'd never seen this side of Madison before, and he had to admit it was hot. Still, there was a lot between them that needed stating out loud and fixing.

"Any chance I can go first? Explain what happened in New York?" he asked.

"Nope." She straddled him and settled into his lap, facing him.

"How about the hearing? Can we talk about that?"

"Eventually."

He blew out a long breath and eased back against the couch, settling in. He figured he'd be here a while. "Go."

"Yeah." She let out a nervous laugh. "I wish it were that easy or simple." She ran a shaking hand through her hair. "I just went to visit Franny. I thought if Eric has his way, it might be the last time, so I wanted to make sure I said everything I could think of. Whether or not she could hear or understand."

His heart twisted for her. And this time, he didn't offer her platitudes, because as she'd learned today, it didn't matter what *should* happen, a judge could rule any way he wanted. Fairness be damned.

"While I was talking to her, she thought I was her sister Gracie … and she was happy. She was in the past and reliving her life, and she laughed and smiled. I thought, *I need to accept that at least she's happy where she is at this moment.* That has to be enough for me. It's certainly enough for her right now."

He smoothed his hand over her hair. "That's huge for you. I'm glad you're finding a way to come to terms with losing her." Because loss was the one thing Madison feared.

"She's not gone. The woman I knew is gone, but another one is here. And you know what? She taught me something today."

Alex caught the twinkle in her eye, and he suddenly had more hope than he'd experienced since seeing her in Ian's conference room that first day.

"What's that?" he asked.

She met his gaze. "Living in the moment has to count. It has to be everything, or I'll have nothing, like you said. It just took seeing Franny happy today to make me realize it."

He waited, sensing she needed to keep going, and he remained silent.

"You're right. I've had a lot of loss. Too much. But here you are, offering me everything in the moment, and I'm so busy worrying about the future that I'm pushing you away. When I could be happy now. *We* could be happy now."

His head began to spin with the possibilities of what she was saying. "So—"

"So…" She drew a deep breath. "I'm here. I'm all in. And now I want to know what the hell you think you were doing with that blonde in New York."

He couldn't help it. He threw his head back and laughed.

She poked him in the stomach with her finger. "Cut that out."

"I was set up." He raised both hands in front of him before she could argue. "I kid you not. My bastard of an agent decided to ambush me with meeting after meeting. He told me this was a test for the job when, in reality, they just wanted to get good publicity shots for the show. He basically told them I'd take the job without my permission. And last night at the restaurant, Allison was in on it. The damned restaurant was loud, she moved in closer. She knew someone was snapping pictures. I didn't."

Madison eyed him, eyes narrowed.

"What? You don't believe me?"

"Of course I believe you. I just can't believe your agent would do something like that to you."

That she trusted his word was huge, and hearing her say it, relief flooded him. "Ex-agent. I fired him as soon as I landed. And I couldn't call you last night or this morning because it was after midnight when I got back to the hotel, and I was up at four for a six a.m. flight."

She nodded. "I didn't like it, but I didn't jump to conclusions. But I was going to call it quits between us."

His gut clenched, and this time, he narrowed his gaze.

"I didn't think I could handle this kind of publicity and the women in your life, waiting for the other shoe to fall and you to decide you were finished with me again."

"Madison," he said on a low growl.

She placed her finger over his lips. "But I realized I can't live waiting to be miserable. That will happen—or it won't. But I need you in my life, and that means getting over my past and my fears."

"I'm here to help you, Angel."

She smiled, but it was far from genuine. "I'm broken, Alex," she said with tears in her eyes. "But I want to get better. I want to get it right with you."

He slid his hand behind her neck and pulled her hair tight. "Let's get one thing straight, okay? There are no other women in my life. None who matter. Want to know why?"

She nodded, staring at him with wide eyes.

"Because I love you. I. Love. You." He said the three words he'd only said to one other woman before, when he'd been nothing more than a kid who didn't know better. He hadn't known what life had in store. Couldn't imagine that this wounded woman who needed him would find a place so deep in his heart he could never let her go.

Madison's breath caught, and a sob escaped. "I love you too." Her throat hurt from holding back tears, but her heart ... that she thought might burst out of her chest.

Those three words meant everything to her. Hours earlier, they might not have been enough to ground her and keep her from leaving. She might not have trusted them. But time with a wise woman who'd lost herself had managed to teach Madison the one lesson she'd desperately needed.

"I love you," she said, wrapping her arms around his neck and pressing her lips to his.

He kissed her back, devouring her mouth, sealing

them together deeply. "You're not getting rid of me, Madison," he promised, separating from her only to pull her against him tightly.

Her cheek rested against his, and she breathed him in. "Whatever happens with the job, we'll make it work. Don't give anything up for me. I promise you, I'm not going anywhere. I know I'll struggle, but I'll work through it."

"No more pulling away? No more giving into fear, right? You have a problem, we talk it out."

She nodded.

"Good. Because I want to give you everything you've never had. Love, trust, a home…"

Another sob rose up in her throat at his words.

"And a family."

She smiled at him. "You already did. Your family accepted me, and I'm so grateful for that."

He pressed his forehead to hers. "I don't mean just *my* family. I mean our family. Yours and mine. I want kids I can teach to throw a baseball and girls who look just like you."

She shook her head back and forth, unable to speak or form a coherent word.

"You don't want kids?" He reared back in shock.

"I do. I just never let myself think about having them. I didn't ever allow myself that dream."

"Well, it's not going to be a dream. It's going to be

our reality. I'm going to make sure of it."

"You're so good to me." She looked into the face of the man she loved, unable to believe life had given them a second chance. Had given her a chance to get her head on straight and not lose the best thing that had ever happened to her.

"We're good together. Don't forget that."

She grinned. "You can be sure I'll remind you … if you ever forget."

"Not likely. Got a question for you now."

She raised an eyebrow.

"Marry me. Make this official."

She blinked at him, stunned, surprised, and overwhelmed. "Are you sure you know what you're getting into?"

"What kind of question is that? For one thing, we belong together. For another, don't you think you'll feel better knowing I want to make a lifetime commitment to you?"

She shook her head. "No. You can't marry me because I have abandonment issues."

He cupped her face in his hand, stroking her cheek with his thumb. "You're right. But I can marry you because *I* have issues with being apart from you in any way. And because I know how I feel. It's a plus that it'll give you even more security. And that's important to me. But binding you to me in every way is exactly what I want."

She shrugged. What else could she say to that? "Yes."

"Yes?"

"Yes."

He grinned and kissed her hard. "Let's go."

"Where?"

"To buy a ring. My fiancée needs to have my ring on her finger."

She smiled. "What kind of female would I be if I said no to that?"

She didn't kid herself that things would be easy or that she wouldn't backslide, but she had the world in her hands and this wonderful man in her life. She'd do everything she could to keep him there. Including fix herself.

*   *   *

Three Months Later

Alex drove toward Ian's house to join his brother at the end of Riley's baby shower. Ian had asked for moral support, and this way, Alex could pick up Madison, who'd gone to the party with some women from work. Alex drove north on I-95, catching sight of the damned billboard with his face plastered there in split screen. Exactly as the PR people had pitched the idea months ago.

He really hadn't wanted to go along with the idea, but a myriad of circumstances had changed his mind. First was Jake, the boy he'd met in New York. They'd become email pals, and at some point, Ian's words about Alex being able to make a difference for kids, and even injured athletes who could be taught to prepare for the future, had gotten to him. And when training camps began over the summer, Alex had begun meeting with the players, both in groups and individually, and he'd come to see the wisdom of the PR campaign. Finally, there was his new TV gig.

When Rachel had called him months ago on behalf of the owners of S&E Network, he hadn't wanted to hear what she had to say. Once again, her persistence had paid off, and he'd been forced to listen. He learned that the setup had been all Allison and his ex-agent's idea. The executives still wanted Alex. He wanted a new cohost. To his shock, they were agreeable.

The show would be Sundays only during football season, which meant his travel time was limited. He was able to keep his job with the Thunder and take on the new opportunity. That was when Madison had approached him again about doing the PR campaign. She believed the new job would be the perfect comeback tool and would bolster the efforts they were doing behind the scenes if coordinated with a public campaign. With Alex as the face of success.

Put like that, he hadn't been able to refuse. If Madison could face her insecurities while he traveled to New York and worked with his female cohost and renewed fame, he could damn well face his own insecurities. Especially if it meant helping others.

Alex pulled his Porsche into the long driveway of his brother's house. He met up with Ian at the front door.

"Eager to escape?" Alex asked, laughing.

"You don't understand what all those drunk women in one room are like," he muttered.

"But Riley can't drink."

"She insisted on mimosas for her friends. Tipsy females giving gifts like breast pumps, nipple cream, and a wiseass one gave her a voucher for a vasectomy. Said she'd be begging me to get one during delivery."

"Ouch, man. That's harsh."

"You're telling me. My brothers left after the first high-pitched screaming laugh." He slapped Alex on the back. "I'm so glad you're here."

"Jesus. Can we stay out here?"

"No way. I've stayed out of their way for the most part, but Riley wants me there for cake and a toast. You can damn well earn your brother stripes and back me up."

"You owe me," Alex muttered, following Ian into the house.

An hour later, Alex was ready to escape the excited women, the tiny-people clothes—how did you hold something that small and not drop it, anyway?—and all those diapers, creams, and instruction books. He was glad he was engaged to be married and had time before he had to face all this … stuff.

He cornered a tipsy Madison in the hall near the kitchen. "Ready to go?" he asked hopefully.

"Another mimosa first." She grabbed his hand and pulled him toward the full bar with a professional mixer Ian had hired.

"Oh, no. I think you've had enough."

She turned toward him. "I haven't. Really. I just think we should stay till the end. For Riley."

He nodded. "Can I get something in exchange for the sacrifice?"

"Such as?" she asked, leaning in close and looping her arms around his neck.

He pulled her into the nearest room and shut the door behind them. "This." He slid his lips over hers and took her mouth, kissing her as if he hadn't seen her and made love to her earlier this morning.

"Mmm. What was that for?"

"Do I need a reason to kiss my soon-to-be wife?" he asked.

"Nope." She threaded her fingers through his hair and refastened her lips over his.

Her tongue glided over his mouth, pushed inside, and she moaned, pulling tighter on his hair and not letting him get away. Not that he wanted to.

With a moan, she finally separated from him. "I've been thinking."

"About?"

"What kind of wedding I want." Before today, Madison had been putting off making a decision on anything to do with the actual ceremony.

Not because she had any doubts but because she didn't know how to have something traditional when her life was anything but. Still, spending the day with a lot of married women talking about babies and families had her ready to make a decision.

Alex grasped her waist in his hands. "Anything you want, it's yours."

She swallowed hard. "I want to be your wife, but I don't want a big wedding with a lot of people. I don't have parents and—"

"No explanations necessary," he assured her.

"I don't want to walk down the aisle alone or with someone who isn't really my father. I just want to marry you. I'd say Las Vegas, but I want your family to be there."

He squeezed her tighter. "And I love you for that. So why not do Vegas? My family can fly out there as easily as we can. Gabe owns a club there. I'm sure he knows all the best places for us to go. It'll be simple."

She stared in surprise. "Really?"

He grinned. "Really."

She blew out a long breath. "Thank you," she said, so relieved he'd agreed. "If Riley can fly, I'd love for her and Ian to be there. If not, I know she'll understand."

He nodded. "I agree."

He was so easy. So special. She stared into those dark chocolate eyes so full of love. For her. She was lucky, she thought not for the first time. Not for the hundredth. He'd turned into the perfect man for her. And throughout the last few months, she'd grown a lot too.

She'd learned to talk to herself during his travels, reassuring herself that his on-air chemistry with the co-host of his show didn't mean he was interested in her. That the other proverbial shoe didn't have to fall. That he didn't have to leave her like others in her life. And thanks to his patience, it was all starting to stick. She was more self-aware, more trusting. And she hoped she could be half the partner for him that he was for her.

"If my family can be there, great. If not … you're all I need, Angel."

"Good thing," she said, smiling. "Because you're all I need too."

EPILOGUE

Gabriel Dare stared at the email he'd received from his cousin Alex. Another Dare male soon to be married. Gabe stared out the window over one of the four terraces in his apartment that overlooked the East River. He had varied business interests, owned the most exclusive nightclubs in the world's most sought-after locations, and he was bored. Not with the business end of things but with his personal life.

The endless available supply of beautiful women did nothing for him. Easy catches didn't stimulate his interest. No, there was only one woman who'd done that lately, and she was living with a pompous ass who didn't deserve her. He ran a hand through his hair, understanding that her lack of availability was for the best.

Gabe had married young and miscalculated badly. He felt responsible for his wife's death, leaving him certain that being alone was his best—his only—

option. One look at *her* had him wanting to do what he always did when hit with a business challenge. Reassess. But matters of the heart had little in common with business, which was more calculated and controlling. He had to put her out of his mind.

Unfortunately, there was something about Isabelle ...

If you missed book 1 in the Dare to Love series, Riley & Ian's story, Dare to Love is available NOW!

Dare to Surrender – Isabelle & Gabe's story available July 15, 2014

Did you enjoy this book? If so, help others enjoy it too. Please recommend to friends and leave a review when possible!

Stay up to date with what's happening with the Dare to Desire series by visiting these links:

My website: www.carlyphillips.com

Sign up for Carly's Newsletter:
http://www.carlyphillips.com/newsletter-sign-up/

Sign up for Blog and Website updates at:
http://www.carlyphillips.com/blog

Sign up for Text Updates of New Releases:
http://tinyurl.com/pbq4fbx

Carly on Facebook:
www.facebook.com/CarlyPhillipsFanPage

Carly on Twitter:
www.twitter.com/carlyphillips

Follow or Friend me on Goodreads:
www.goodreads.com/author/show/10000.Carly_Phillips

CARLY'S MONTHLY CONTEST!

Every month I run a contest at my website – Visit:
http://www.carlyphillips.com/newsletter-sign-up/
and enter for a chance to win a $25 gift card! You'll also automatically be added to my newsletter list so you can keep up on my newest releases!"

Read on for an excerpt from my upcoming book, DARE TO SURRENDER.

Dare to Surrender – Excerpt

Isabelle: Out of the Frying Pan

I was arrested a mile outside of Manhattan. Grand theft auto, the cop said. Bullshit, I replied. The baby Benz belonged to me.

Still, he cuffed me and hauled me to the nearest police station. He said his name was Officer Dare and he was a dark haired man, tall, taller than Lance, who prided himself on his height, and broader from what I could tell beneath his uniform. His intense expression never wavered. All seriousness, all the time, but I sensed he'd be handsome if he smiled. So far, he hadn't.

Once inside the typical looking police station – not that I'd seen the inside of one before – but what I'd thought one would look like from Law and Order – he sat me beside his wooden desk, and *cuffed* me to the desk!

I ought to be scared but some stupid part of me had already decided this new part of my life was some grand adventure. At least it was until Officer Dare asked me to empty my pockets and divested me of my last $500 dollars, cash I'd taken from the *extra* stash I kept in my nightstand.

He thumbed through the bulging stack of twenties in never ending silence.

The money represented my lifeline. "I'll need to eat when I get out of here," I told my jailer.

He didn't look up. "You'll get it back."

"All of it?" I asked, as if I seriously believed a member of the police force would take a *down on their luck* woman's chance at food.

He set his jaw in annoyance. "We log it and count it. In front of you. I was just about to do that … Ma'am."

For some inane reason, I burst out laughing. I'd gone from living in denial to homeless and arrested in a ridiculously short time. This whole turn in my life really was absurd.

I rubbed my free hand up and down over one arm. "Don't I get one phone call?"

He nodded and reached for the telephone on the desk.

I frowned, suddenly realizing I had no one to call. Lance was out of the question and *our* friends were really *his* friends. As for my parents, they didn't remember my birthday, so something told me a late night call to pick up their daughter from jail would not be their number one priority.

"Never mind," I said softly.

The officer stared at me, confused. "Now you

281

don't want to use the phone?"

"No thank you." Because I was totally, utterly alone.

Nausea rose like bile in my throat and I dug my nails into my palms. When I forced myself to breath deeply, the familiar burning in my chest returned and I realized I'd walked away without the one thing I never left home without and it wasn't my license.

"Any chance you've got some Tums?" I asked.

He ground his teeth together and I swear I heard his molars scraping. "Okay, yeah. I'll get right on that," he muttered and strode off.

"I'll just wait here," I called back. I lifted my arm the short distance the cuffs would allow and groaned.

What felt like an endless stretch of time passed during which I reviewed my options, of which, once again, I had none.

Now what, I wondered, utter and complete despair threatening for the first time. Eventually I swallowed back the lump in my throat and forced myself to make the best of the situation.

I kicked my feet against the linoleum floor. Leaned back in the chair and studied the cracked ceiling. Hummed along to the tune crackling on the radio in the background. And yeah, I tried not to cry.

"You know, I thought it would take me longer to get you in cuffs." A familiar masculine voice that oozed pure sin sounded beside me.

It couldn't be, I thought, but from the tingling in my body, I already knew it was. "Gabriel Dare, what brings you into this part of Mayberry?"

He chuckled, a deeply erotic sound that matched his mention of the handcuffs, but he didn't answer my question.

Left with no choice, I tipped my head and looked into his self-possessed, dark blue, eyes. Eyes too similar to my cop and suddenly the last name registered. In an unfamiliar place and time, my mind on my arrest and nothing more, I hadn't made the connection before.

I knew Gabriel Dare from the country club Lance belonged to but despite the upper crust connection, there was nothing similar about the two men. Where Lance was sandy haired and a touch Waspish in looks, Gabe, as his friends called him, possessed thick, dark sable hair and roguish good looks.

Gabe's very posture and demeanor set him apart from any other man I'd met. His white teeth, tanned skin, and chiseled features were put together in a way that made him extraordinarily handsome. That he owned the space and air around him merely added to his appeal. An appeal that had never been lost on me, not even now, shackled as I was to a desk in a police station.

His stare never wavered, those navy eyes locked on me and if I hadn't been sitting, I'd be in a puddle at his feet.

"You look good cuffed," he said in a deliciously low voice.

Immediate thoughts of me bound and at his mercy assaulted me. My body, which hadn't been worshiped well in far too long, if ever, had been taken over by the notion of Gabe, his strong touch playing me with an expert hand.

I squeezed my thighs together, but instead of easing, the ache only grew. Heat rushed through me at a rapid pace, my breasts heavy, my sex pulsing in a dull throbbing that begged to be filled. I blinked hard in an impossible attempt to center myself.

He grinned, as if he'd heard every naughty thought in my head.

It had always been this way between us. Any time I ran into him at the club, the attraction had been electric and when we found ourselves alone, the flirting outrageous.

One night Gabe caught me exiting the Ladies' Room. Lance came upon us then and once home, he'd accused me of desiring Gabe. I'd denied it, of course.

I'd lied.

Lance knew it and after catching us talking privately at more than one event, he'd kept a firm lock on my arm. And because I desperately wanted the life I'd chosen to make sense, I'd allowed the possession.

Besides, Gabe always had an elegant woman on his arm, a different one each time. He could have any beautiful female he desired. Why would he choose me? Even Lance, who I'd been with for what felt like a lifetime, liked ownership, not *me*. And let's face it, my parents hadn't wanted me either. So believing in myself wasn't my strong suit.

"So. What are you in for?" Gabe settled in his brother's chair, propping an elbow on the cluttered desk so he could lean closer. "Prostitution?"

"Excuse me?" I choked out. "You know I'm not a hooker!" I said offended, the whispers I'd heard when Lance and I first got together, rushing back.

Gold digger and mistress were among the chosen words, never mind that Lance's single-minded pursuit had broken down every one of my defenses.

Gabe chuckled, assuring me he'd been joking. "Seriously, you dress down as well as you dress up." His gaze raked over me, hot approval in the inky depths, appreciating me in a way Lance never had.

My insides trembled at the overwhelming effect this man had over me. "Where's the cop with my money?" I asked, glancing around.

"Worried about your stash?" Gabe drummed his fingers on the desk. "Are you sure you're not a hooker?" he mused.

I didn't want to grin but I did. "Why are you so desperate to think I am? Are you a pimp or something?"

He burst out laughing, the sound echoing through the walls of the quiet station. "Not quite," he said, obviously amused.

The tread of his brother's heavy footsteps announced his return.

Gabe looked at the other man with a disappointed expression. "Bro, didn't anyone tell you you're supposed to handcuff a lady to the headboard, not a desk?" He folded his arms across his broad chest. "It's no wonder you can't get any action."

I ducked my head, trying not to laugh …

Dare to Surrender – Isabelle & Gabe's story
available July 15, 2014

About the Author

N.Y. *Times* and *USA Today* Bestselling Author Carly Phillips has written over 40 sexy contemporary romance novels. After a successful 15 year career with various New York publishing houses, Carly made the leap to Indie author, with the goal of giving her readers more books at a faster pace at a better price. Carly lives in Purchase, NY with her family, two nearly adult daughters and two crazy dogs who star on her Facebook Fan Page and website. She's a writer, a knitter of sorts, a wife, and a mom. In addition, she's a Twitter and Internet junkie and is always around to interact with her readers.

CARLY'S BOOKLIST
by Series

Below are links to my series on my website where you will find buy links for each novel!

Dare to Love Series

http://www.carlyphillips.com/category/books/?series=dare-to-love

Dare to Love

Dare to Desire

Dare to Surrender

Serendipity Series

http://www.carlyphillips.com/category/books/?series=serendipity-series

Serendipity

Destiny

Karma

Serendipity's Finest Series

http://www.carlyphillips.com/category/books/?series=serendipitys-finest

Perfect Fit

Perfect Fling

Perfect Together

Serendipity Novellas

http://www.carlyphillips.com/category/books/?series=serendipity-novellas

Kismet

Fated

Hot Summer Nights (Perfect Stranger)

Bachelor Blog Series
http://www.carlyphillips.com/category/books/?series=bachelor-blog-series
Kiss Me If You Can
Love Me If You Dare

Lucky Series
http://www.carlyphillips.com/category/books/?series=lucky-series
Lucky Charm
Lucky Streak
Lucky Break

Ty and Hunter Series
http://www.carlyphillips.com/category/books/?series=ty-hunter-series
Cross My Heart
Sealed with a Kiss

Hot Zone Series
http://www.carlyphillips.com/category/books/?series=hot-zone-series
Hot Stuff
Hot Number
Hot Item
Hot Property

Costas Sisters Series
http://www.carlyphillips.com/category/books/?series=costas-sisters-series
Summer Lovin'
Under the Boardwalk

Chandler Brothers Series

http://www.carlyphillips.com/category/books/?series=chandler-brothers-series

The Bachelor

The Playboy

The Heartbreaker

Stand Alone Titles

http://www.carlyphillips.com/category/books/?series=other-books

Brazen

Seduce Me

Secret Fantasy

Love Unexpected Series

http://www.carlyphillips.com/category/books/?series=ebooks

Perfect Partners

Solitary Man

The Right Choice

Midnight Angel

Anthologies

http://www.carlyphillips.com/category/books/?series=anthologies

Truly Madly Deeply (boxed set of Perfect Partners, The Right Choice, Solitary Man)

Sinfully Sweet (also includes The Right Choice and 5 other authors)

More Than Words Volume 7

Santa Baby (Carly's Naughty or Nice novella)

Invitations to Seduction (Carly's Going All the Way – not in print)

CPSIA information can be obtained at www.ICGtesting.com
Printed in the USA
LVOW08s0927041014

407286LV00016B/465/P